RIVER OF DREAMS

A NOVEL

Daniel Linden Duke

Published By: Daniel Linden Duke

ISBN 978-1-964452-57-9 (HardCover)
ISBN 979-8-88793-577-5 (SoftCover)
ISBN 978-1-964452-59-3 (Digital)

2025908855 (Library of Congress Control Number)

Printed in the United States of America

Novels by the Author

Man Camp

Pursuit of Happiness

Serenity

River of Dreams

Visit the author's website at https://daniellindenduke.com

Dedication

To Cheryl: I can neither imagine nor hope for a more perfect person with whom to share my life.

Chapter 1

A Remarkable Story to Share

If you'll pardon the indelicacy, a good story is a lot like flatulence. It cannot be withheld indefinitely. I've waited almost three decades to share the story that follows. Respect for patient privacy and personal friendship compelled me to do so. Now that Emory Allen Ashcroft III has celebrated his homegoing, as they say in these parts, I am finally at liberty to proceed. As you've probably guessed, I'm not a storyteller by trade. Until recently bread got put on my table because I tended to folks' aches and pains. Occasionally I also brought someone into this world or ushered them out. It was in the course of performing my medical duties, in fact, that I became entangled in the lives and events that make up a large part of my story.

One person's story, of course, can be another's sedative. Doubtless some readers will find my story a trifle domestic. Cravers of thrills and action addicts might do well to read no further. Those on whose upright shoulders the burdens of age have yet to fall also may not find this story to their liking. The kind of person, I think, who is most apt to enjoy what follows is someone who's floated around a while at the confluence of destiny and coincidence, the sort of individual who has grappled with the currents that drag folks in a particular direction and who understands their struggles to change course.

A story without a setting is no more complete than a breath without an exhalation. My story is set in the country bordering the James River, that tireless treadmill of Virginia history. The river's many twists and curls match the course of the tale I'm about to tell. Rivers frequently are endowed with colorful nicknames. The Mississippi is "Big Muddy" and "the Father of Waters." The Yellow River is "China's Sorrow." Virginians, either because they lack the imagination gene or, more likely, they possess a perverse desire to be different, simply refer to the James River as the James River, the James, or the River (pronounced "Rivuh"). If anyone asked me, which of course no one has, I'd suggest calling the James the "River of Dreams."

Dreams of great wealth brought the first English settlers to the River. When these dreams faded, yeoman colonists followed, each hoping to become an independent landowner. The shores of the James have witnessed more than one ardent group of rebels struggle to achieve their dreams. Less than three score years after the first whites arrived at Jamestown, Nathaniel Bacon torched the settlement in a vain effort to break free of His Majesty's yoke. Rebellious colonists living along the banks of the James helped to set in motion the events leading to the Revolutionary War. When the Confederacy rose in defense of slavery, General George McClellan led a huge army to the land along the James in the hopes of scoring a decisive victory and thereby bringing a swift end to the Civil War. A century later Yankees returned to the James, this time seeking respite from urban sprawl. They nested in plantation-like splendor behind gated entrances and beside lush fairways.

A dream imagined is not necessarily a dream realized. The lowlands along the James have sucked down their share of noble as well as ignoble ambitions. Opechancanough's vision of a mighty tribal alliance gave way to the colonists' insatiable desire for land. For every planter who wrestled fortune from the swamps, an unmarked grave claimed the bones of another who failed. Countrymen fought and killed each other here, mixing their blood with the murky waters of the James. Even the most recent pilgrims have been known to repack their belongings and leave, disappointed that the promise of pastoral retirement in the Old Dominion attracted too many others with similar desires.

The story I want to tell you did not take place along the entire 335-mile length of the James River. Rather, it is limited to a stretch of the River bookended by Jamestown to the east and Richmond to the west. An odd assortment of "volumes" occupies the space in between: leather-bound classics, dime-store novels, and unfinished memoirs. I've heard this area referred to in various ways. One pundit called it "a land of hope, hate, and habit." Historians consider this low country to be the birthplace of the United States and its democratic form of government. The future of our nation was threatened and eventually secured here, not once but twice. The North American origins of that "peculiar institution" known as slavery can be traced to the shores of the James, as can a cornucopia of our favorite virtues and vices. Despite the bogus claims of our northern brothers and sisters, the first Thanksgiving in the New World took place here in 1619 at Berkeley Plantation. The first college in the New World was planned for Henricus, near the present city of Hopewell, but never completed. Other firsts include the first Christian conversion of a Native American, the first cultivation of tobacco for commercial purposes, and, of particular interest to this storyteller, the first distilling of bourbon whiskey.

Charles City County, named in honor of the ill-fated King Charles I, is the region's heart, my adopted home, and the principal site of my story. Located twelve miles southeast of Richmond, Charles City County is a mere thirteen miles long and eight miles wide, yet within its borders has occurred enough history to make a high school student gag. First impressions of the place depend a great deal on how you approach it. If you come by boat, you catch glimpses of stately Queen Anne and Georgian mansions flanked by boxwood-bordered gardens and fertile fields. If you drive along the John Tyler Highway, Route 5, Charles City County seems to consist of a scattering of modest homes, small farms, and abandoned outbuildings. If you get adventurous and wander the secondary roads that weave through the area, you find yourself in the midst of scrub pine and swamp, small African-American settlements of considerable age, homeless chimneys and overgrown family burial plots. If there's anything lonelier looking than a solitary brick chimney or a family plot with no living family nearby, I can't think of what it would be.

Were you raised in the distant highlands, you might be struck by the relationship between topography and social status in these parts. When rivers run through hill country, poverty hugs the river banks. The further from the river folks live, the better off they're likely to be. Not so in the lowlands. A view of the River is regarded as a birthright by the well-to-do. Of course, I'll admit that there are probably some people who object to the view, at least the vista from the north bank of the James. You see, a case can be made that the real Dixie, the South of slow drawls and deep prejudices, begins on the southern banks of the James. As for me, about the only thing across the River that I don't particularly care for these days is the Surry nuclear power plant. If you question my sympathies, let me declare before we go any further that I'm not one of those "lost cause" lunatics who claims he's a reluctant citizen of the Re-united States of America and who refuses to purchase a blue automobile. What's done is done. Staring at the rearview mirror is a lousy way to move forward.

I'm not sure the central character of my story would agree with my last statement. Emory Ashcroft was born and raised within a five iron of the James, and the River's history is closely intertwined with the history of his family. Ashcroft maintained that the land of his birth possessed a deceptive quality. The view from the River obscured the abject poverty inland. The view from Route 5, on the other hand, concealed any hint of the luxury that lined the River. Ashcroft liked to add, "What else would you expect of a place named Charles City County that has no city?" As rural as a place can be, the closest thing to a county center is a tiny courthouse along Route 5. Behind the brick courthouse, which dates back to around 1730, stands a more recently erected obelisk honoring local men who fought for the Confederacy. Inscribed on the obelisk are the words, "Defenders of Constitutional Liberty and the Right of Self Government." Black and Native American residents of Charles City County, along with a growing number of Whites, rightfully dispute the accuracy of the inscription.

Any hope that Charles City County would regain a measure of its colonial and antebellum importance evaporated with the opening of Interstate 64. In the hour or so it takes to zip from Richmond to Hampton Roads, travelers with no reason to tarry catch no glimpse of the James River, the battlefields of the Peninsula Campaign – known in these parts as the Seven Days, and the graceful plantations that housed two Presidents and a host of other luminaries. Charles City County has become one of those places referred to more in the past tense than the present tense. Neighboring counties have fared better, thanks to new cash crops – tourists and retirees. Between upscale subdivisions catering to senior citizens and the history-rich triangle formed by Williamsburg, Jamestown, and Yorktown, the past literally has become the region's future.

So this is the place to which I'd like to invite you, a place I've been honored to call home for three decades. Pull up a comfortable chair, pour yourself a glass of good sipping bourbon, and let me tell you a most unusual tale.

Chapter 2

THE ASHCROFTS OF CHARLES CITY COUNTY

My name is Russell Curry, but most everyone calls me Doc. I don't discourage this informality because I was never all that keen about my Christian name. Even though I sold my practice to a bright young woman from Baltimore several months ago, people continue to call me Doc. Truth be told, I never would have discovered what I'm about to share with you had I not moved my medical practice from Richmond to Charles City County. How I came to do so is a story in itself, one I'd just as soon forget. Suffice it to say that after finishing medical school at Mr. Jefferson's University and completing my residency at the Medical College of Virginia, I married well. When you marry well in Richmond and it doesn't work out, you always divorce badly.

My ex-wife was Old Richmond, the daughter and granddaughter and great granddaughter of prominent lawyers and legislators. She was Windsor Farms; I was Patterson Avenue. Her family buried at Hollywood; my family buried at Forest Lawn. After we split, I figured it might be best for my practice as well as my ego to change venue. When I ran across Tobias Galloway's advertisement for a medical partner, someone who might eventually take over his practice, I jumped at the opportunity. That's how I came to Charles City County in 1966, just in time to celebrate the county's

350th anniversary. Understandably, I was not inclined to join in the local celebrations.

Almost a decade would pass before I met Emory Ashcroft. I might never have met him if Doc Galloway's buddies hadn't convinced him that April was the perfect time for a Pinehurst golf vacation. There I was, alone in the office, the nurse and receptionist having left for the day, when the phone rang. You know how you can have an inkling about certain phone calls? I actually hesitated to pick up the receiver because that little voice in my head told me this was no routine call from a drug salesman or a patient needing to make an appointment. All I really wanted to do was lock up and go home.

The voice on the other end of the line had not spoken a dozen words before I knew that this was a voice I could listen to for a long time, a very long time. What appealed to me had less to do with the words themselves than the elegant pacing and gracious tone. "I'm so sorry to call after hours. Is this Tobias? Oh! Please pardon me, Doctor Curry. This is Gray Ashcroft. We've not met, but I have heard wonderful things about you. Is Tobias there? Well, it's about time he got away for some relaxation. Could I prevail on you, Doctor Curry, to look in on my husband? I must visit my daughter in California, and I'm concerned about Emory, that's my husband. If you'd care to drop by for a glass of sherry, I could explain more before I leave."

Had anyone else phoned with such a request, I would have responded that house calls in Virginia went out with the Byrd Machine and that I'd be glad to set up an office appointment. Instead, I asked for directions. Directions, though, were hardly necessary. Everyone in Charles City County, even a relative newcomer like myself, knew where Gray and Emory Ashcroft lived. Their plantation, Devon, was a local landmark, one of the oldest estates on the James.

Before I continue, I should explain that my medical partner's enthusiasm for relinquishing his practice cooled markedly after my arrival. This reaction had less to do with my competence than with Tobias' fear over how he would occupy himself once he'd been "pastured." While I was assigned all the new patients, the Medicaid patients, and a smattering of old-timers, Tobias clung to his well-heeled "river people" the way Virginia clay sticks to your shoes after a good rain. I imagined he would be more than a little put out when he learned that I had been called to the Ashcrofts in his absence.

The Ashcrofts lived off Route 5, just east of Charles City County's best known plantations, Berkeley and Shirley. As I passed between the pineapple-capped brick posts that marked the entrance to Ashcroft property, I expected the mansion would appear around the first bend in the road. Instead, I drove on for ten minutes, passing pine forests, fallow fields, fields under cultivation, mostly corn and soy beans, an orchard, various farm structures, a Georgian-style stable half the length of a football field, grape arbors, several kitchen gardens, a cluster of ancient dependencies, and a formal garden bordered by eight-foot-high boxwoods. Finally I reached the heart of the estate, a three-story Georgian mansion of brick flanked on each side by a two-story addition with wood siding. The place reminded me of a slightly smaller version of Westover, William Byrd the Second's grand outpost on the James. Just as arresting as the initial view of Devon was the panorama it commanded. Someone sipping bourbon on the front lawn could see several miles up river and down river. I parked my Jeep Wagoneer in the carriageway that circled in front of the entrance and savored the setting for several seconds before getting out.

With a new patient, I tend to begin by taking in the entire person before me, then following up with a closer inspection of anything out of the ordinary. I do something similar when visiting a new place. Thus it was that my initial impression of Devon required some adjustment once I left my vehicle and examined the main house more carefully. Hints of neglect were abundant. Broken slats and peeling paint were visible on the second and third floor shutters. The massive chimneys required pointing up. A number of roof slates were chipped and cracked. Before I could complete my inspection, however, the voice I had heard on the phone called out from the side of the house. "Doctor Curry, how very wonderful of you to be so prompt. I always say that a man who knows how to be on time is a man worth spending time with."

Half-expecting to see a silver-haired doyenne in bonnet and hoop skirt, I turned toward the voice. My eyes instead embraced a fetching blond in a low-cut pastel sundress and sandals. Sunglasses were pushed back on top of her head, revealing eyes the color of Delft china. Her hair was pulled back in a ponytail, reminding me of the girls with whom I went to high school, but their innocent beauty presented awkwardly, not with the casual elegance of the woman before me. In her right hand she cradled a champagne flute, while her left hand held a basket of fresh-cut flowers. The word "stunning" probably was coined to capture the effect of a woman like this. I appreciated what a deer must feel like when it freezes before an automobile's headlights. How old could she be,

I wondered.

My failure to respond seemed to puzzle my host. She looked down at her glass, then said apologetically, "Forgive me, Doctor Curry. I'm Gray Ashcroft. I find that a little champagne makes gardening much easier."

"Please call me Russell," I responded, regretting that I was not blessed with a more aristocratic name. My mother had insisted that I be named after her older brother, who went to New York City to become an actor and died in his early twenties after a homeopathic quack failed to detect a serious infection. I suspect that her brother, not my father, was the true love of her life.

Mrs. Ashcroft set down her glass and flower basket in order to shake my hand. "I must admit I expected a much older man. If I didn't know better, I'd swear I was greeting Paul Newman. Is this your first visit to Devon?"

I nodded that it was, but thought her question odd. Wouldn't she have known if I'd previously visited?

Mrs. Ashcroft thanked me to the point of embarrassment for making a house call and admitted that her husband would never dream of visiting a physician's office unless he was staring the grim reaper in the face. I asked why she was so concerned about her husband, and she lowered her voice to tell me that he was under enormous pressure and had been for months. From what I could gather, Devon once had been a thriving farm producing a variety of cash crops, but inflation had taken its toll. Keeping up with rising costs for labor, equipment, repairs, and gasoline compelled the Ashcrofts to borrow a considerable sum at high interest rates. The farm was not producing enough to pay the interest, much less the principal.

I felt uncomfortable hearing about the Ashcrofts' financial circumstances, and it surprised me that Mrs. Ashcroft would be so forthcoming with a stranger. Virginians will talk about a great many things, but family finances is not one of them. Dealing with my ex-wife's clan taught me that the Old Dominion's aristocracy was far too proud to admit error, ignorance, and fiscal failure.

"Is your husband in good health generally?" I asked, trying to change the subject.

A touch of arthritis was all he complained about, according to my informant, but she was certain he kept a lot bottled up inside. Turning her back to me, she gazed at the River.

"This plantation has been in Emory's family for over 300 years, Doctor Curry." I liked the way she pronounced her husband's name, dropping the "o" and lingering over the first syllable. "Devon has never ceased to be a working farm, not during the Revolutionary War, not during the War Between the States, not during the terrible drought of 1930, not even during the height of the Great Depression. Emory can't help thinking it'll all come to an end on his watch."

Were the Ashcrofts' financial straits really as serious as she indicated? Mrs. Ashcroft must have sensed what I was thinking because she turned around and told me that I needed to talk with her husband about the future of Devon. "You're probably imagining that I've been exaggerating, Doctor Curry. But if I know anything in this fickle world, it's Emory Ashcroft. You earned your MD. Well, I earned an advanced degree in my husband. If I weren't going away, I would not be overly concerned, but I must visit my daughter on the West Coast. Emory is not accustomed to being on his own."

Gently touching my elbow, Mrs. Ashcroft guided me up the front steps and into the great center hall that ran, as was customary in Georgian mansions, the entire width of the house. Age-darkened portraits in heavy gilded frames lined the oak-paneled walls. Midway down the hall an ornate staircase flanked by additional portraits ascended gracefully to the second floor. At the far end of the center hall, a large screen door revealed a veranda, gardens, and the River. A fragrant and refreshing breeze flowed from back door to front door. Four massive rooms, two on each side, bordered the center hall. Mrs. Ashcroft invited me into one, a combination library and sitting room lined with floor-to-ceiling bookshelves and filled with over-stuffed chairs. A substantial stone fireplace occupied the south wall, and above it hung another portrait.

"That's the first Emory Allen Ashcroft, my Emory's great grandfather," Mrs. Ashcroft explained as she motioned for me to have a seat. "Reputedly an amazing man. You'll have to get Emory to tell you all about him. If there's one thing my husband loves, it's recounting his family history." The soft cushioning of my chair absorbed me as my host excused herself. "Do make yourself comfortable, Doctor Curry."

"Russell."

"Yes, Russell it will be from now on. I won't be a minute. Emory's probably walking Jeb."

I tried to rise, out of politeness, but my first effort was unsuccessful. By the time I overcame the gravitational pull of my chair, Mrs. Ashcroft had departed to find her husband.

Whether I dozed off or simply closed my eyes for a moment, I can't recall. What I do remember is being startled when a large dog placed both its front paws on my lap and licked my face.

"Down, Jeb. Christ-a-mighty, dog, get off the man!" A slender, tanned arm reached down and grabbed the dog's collar, yanking him away. "Doctor Curry, please excuse my friend here. I'm afraid he laid claim to your chair years ago."

I looked up to see a tall man, slightly stooped in the manner of Gary Cooper and Jimmy Stewart, wearing khaki pants and a blue button-down oxford shirt. Had it not been for the weathered face, he could have passed for a college student. Trim, athletic, blessed with a brilliant smile and finely chiseled features, the third Emory Allen Ashcroft would have been a perfect understudy for one of those leading men from the forties and fifties over whom demure women secretly swooned. I guess I had imagined – or maybe hoped – that a woman as striking as Mrs. Ashcroft had settled for a feeble old geezer with a pedigree who was content to bask in his young wife's reflected light.

"Permit me to apologize for the lamentable condition of my estate," Mr. Ashcroft said as he shook my hand.

Before I could respond, Mrs. Ashcroft interjected, "Emory, the good doctor here only consented to waste his valuable time with you if you plied him with sherry."

"Surely you can't be serious, my dear. No self-respecting Virginia gentleman would accept anything less than bourbon. What can I offer you, Doctor Curry."

"Please don't take offense, Mrs. Ashcroft," I responded. "Sherry is lovely, but I was born and raised in the Old Dominion and I believe I qualify as a gentleman, so I am compelled by birth and temperament to request bourbon. Straight up, if you don't mind."

"I like this man already," Mr. Ashcroft said as he walked over to a serving cart containing several bottles, assorted glasses, a silver ice bucket, and other bartending accoutrement.

Claiming that she needed to finish her gardening chores, Mrs. Ashcroft turned down her husband's offer of a drink. With Garden Week just around the corner, she wanted to make certain her plantings were not in the "deplorable" condition they had been in the previous spring. After she left, Mr. Ashcroft explained, "Gray does an estimable job, Russell, but there's just too much for one person to take care of. We used to have three gardeners throughout the spring and summer. Gray called them her Corps des Jardin."

An awkward pause followed as each of us sipped our bourbon. I wondered how best to broach the subject of my host's mental state. Emory Ashcroft clearly was gracious, but I suspected he was also a proud and self-reliant man. Any suggestion that he might not be up to handling affairs at Devon during his wife's absence could provoke him and destroy any chance for me to provide professional help. It would be best, I reckoned, if I took Mrs. Ashcroft's advice and expressed an interest in Devon's history.

That Mr. Ashcroft harbored strong feelings for his heritage was quickly confirmed by his delighted reaction to my request. For the next hour, Emory – he insisted I drop any formality – shared the official version of his family history. I say "official" because he obviously had given the same lecture countless times. There was just the right amount of pepper with the salt. Emory offered enough evidence, typically accompanied by a wink or a toast, to demonstrate that he was hardly descended from saints, but not enough damning detail to provoke outright condemnation of any particular ancestor or suggest that the Ashcroft clan deserved anything less than a rightful place in Virginia's FFV pantheon.

The closest I got to any real insight into Emory's world was when he offered to refill my glass, and I accepted. He must have expected me to decline, for he interrupted his lecture long enough to tell me that his parents introduced him to bourbon at the tender age of 15. As he put it, "I was raised to be suspicious of people who drank too much and people who didn't drink at all. Both were reprehensible, particularly teetotalers. My father believed that it was a man's sacred duty to hold his liquor, especially in public." After this comment, Emory paused to let Jeb lick the last drops of bourbon from his glass.

Emory's account of his family history began with Oliver Cromwell's rise to power in England. Sensing that the royalist cause was doomed, James Ashcroft sold off a sizeable chunk of family property in Devonshire and moved to Virginia. By the time Charles I was beheaded and Cromwell had converted England to a sober Presbyterian stronghold, James Ashcroft had patented 1500 acres along the James River and christened it Devon, after his birthplace. Emory took obvious pride in the fact that the Virginia colony managed to remain royalist during Cromwell's regime, even rejecting advice from its New World neighbors in Massachusetts to bend to the will of the "roundhead fanatic."

After Cromwell's death and the resignation of his son, Richard, Parliament restored the monarchy and invited Charles II to return to England. Virginia, Emory pointed out, recognized Charles II as king before Parliament actually extended the invitation. Loyalty had its rewards, as the Ashcrofts and their fellow royalists soon discovered. While Charles II proved to be a frivolous monarch and no friend of the yeoman farmer in England or Virginia, he did not turn his back on the wealthy planters. Their influence, like their crops, thrived in the fertile lowlands along the James. Devon almost doubled in size, thanks to the labor of nearly a hundred enslaved workers and London's insatiable desire for Virginia tobacco. Other than fine fabric and heirloom-quality furniture, Devon produced virtually everything necessary to live a genteel life. Residents of the great houses that lined the James River gathered at each other's homes for parties, politics, and courting. The economic value of Devon's tobacco, corn, and cotton, according to Emory's account, was exceeded only by the financial benefits that accrued from marrying off Ashcroft offspring.

Emory supplemented his lecture by escorting me around the mansion, pointing out portraits of ancestors to whom he had referred and curios associated with their lives. That my host derived great honor from his ancestral connections was clear, but even more obvious was his devotion to compiling and sharing the family's history. The older I get, the more I admire the efforts of folks like Emory to preserve their ancestral past. If they choose to varnish these accounts a bit, I'm not offended. The urge to pursue the truth at whatever cost that consumes so many scholars these days has never impressed me very much. If you ask me, most accounts purported to be "true" turn out to be fabricated in one way or another. I had an old professor at Mr. Jefferson's University who used to say, "You're apt to find more truth in fiction and more fiction in truth when you get to be my age."

My apologies. These opinions are hardly of importance. It is discourteous of me to repay your attention by indulging my vanity. All I really meant to say is that I'll take a good story over an academic treatise any day.

By the time the colonists began thinking about throwing off England's oppressive yoke, the Ashcrofts had become one of Virginia's leading families. Emory intimated that his ancestors probably were not especially keen to sever ties with their homeland, but they had a gift for anticipating the inevitable. Just as their forebears sensed that Cromwell's experiment would be short-lived, the Ashcrofts of the late 18th Century realized that Virginia and her fellow colonies were destined to be free. Rejecting overtures from their Tory friends to return to England or migrate to Canada, the Ashcrofts let it be known that they supported self-government for the colonies. They also let it be known that they were more than willing, for a fair price, to help provision colonial militias. During the Revolutionary War, Devon's hospitality was enjoyed by the likes of George Washington and Thomas Jefferson. Rumor had it that several high-ranking English officers also found respite at the plantation.

The cessation of hostilities in 1783 found no slow-down in the family's accumulation of wealth. Eschewing entreaties to become active in the new state and federal governments, Ashcroft men preferred to continue doing what they did best: managing Devon and making money. They steadily diversified, relying less and less on tobacco and cotton and more on corn, wheat, and livestock. With the acquisition of additional land came the purchase of more human beings. Emory was careful to note that Devon's enslaved population received "decent treatment" from his forebears, as evidenced by the absence of any recorded uprisings or attempted escapes. There was even a small school where enslaved house workers were taught to read the Bible, one of only two such facilities in all of antebellum Virginia. To Emory's credit, however, he made no attempt to justify the enslavement of human beings or consider the practice anything other than an abomination.

By the time Emory's great grandfather and namesake, the first Emory Allen Ashcroft, assumed control of Devon in 1859, the thirty-year-old presided over as fine an estate as any in the Old Dominion. Devon's horses, whiskey, and hardwood were highly coveted commodities at home and abroad. Not even the cataclysmic War Between the States diminished the Ashcrofts' prospects. Though Devon wound up in the midst of McClellan's Peninsula Campaign in the summer of 1862, the plantation hardly suffered a scratch, due in large part to the presence of a Union field hospital on the premises. As soon as Robert E. Lee forced McClellan to abandon his run on Richmond, Emory's great grandfather had the pineapple finial removed from Devon's roof. According to legend, he had no desire to provide any more hospitality to Yankees. Provisions from Devon's fields, forests, and streams helped sustain the Army of Northern Virginia right up to the evacuation of Richmond in 1865. Dr. Hunter Maguire, the renowned Confederate physician, even asked Emory Ashcroft to grow opium poppies because his surgeons were short on narcotics.

The fortunes of the Ashcrofts ebbed after the war, as Emory's ancestors learned the meaning of land-rich and cash-poor. No longer able to rely on enslaved workers, the Ashcrofts were compelled to find sharecroppers and hired hands. Many able-bodied men were lured away from Charles City County to work on expanding railroad systems. In order to raise money to pay farm hands a competitive wage, parts of the plantation had to be auctioned. As mechanical farm equipment began to replace human muscle, additional funds were required. Devon shrank back to its original 300 acres. As a point of honor, the Ashcrofts refused to sell land to anyone but Southerners, preferably Virginians listed in the social register. Emory's great grandfather let it be known that he'd "sooner sacrifice my first-born than sell to a carpetbagger." When a Yankee journalist asked him if he were a "true Virginia blue-blood," he reputedly snapped back, "My blood, sir, runs gray, not blue."

Throughout the last part of the 19th Century and the beginning of the 20th, the Ashcrofts struggled to regain their financial footing. No such struggle was required, though, where social status was concerned. With many of Virginia's first families facing financial hardship, there arose in the ranks an unwritten understanding that social standing superseded wealth in importance. Emory's grandfather, Emory Allen Ashcroft, Jr., parlayed the family name into a seat in the Virginia General Assembly at the tender age of thirty-five. His brother, Jefferson Randolph Ashcroft, having given his life at Gettysburg for the Lost Cause, earned the family additional social credit. Every July 3, Ashcroft men retired to Devon's library after dinner to drink a solemn toast to Colonel Ashcroft and "all those who fell by his side."

As the railroads pushed west, more agricultural products from mid-western farms moved into markets once dominated by Southern farmers. Remaining competitive was a challenge, but one to which the Ashcrofts rose. Through diversification, crop rotation, and what some neighbors alleged were strong-arm tactics with local merchants, Emory's grandfather slowly replenished the family coffers. The old man, in fact, was on the verge of buying back parcels of Devon's auctioned acreage when the drought of 1930 struck like a Yankee fusillade. Parts of the James looked more like the Apian Way than a great river. Neighbors refused to share well water. Each day brought bitter news of another farm sale or foreclosure.

During this trying time, Emory's father, Mosby Martin Ashcroft, proved that he had inherited his clan's knack for shrewd financial judgment. Taking over the day-to-day management of Devon from his aging and increasingly distracted father, Mosby enacted a variety of cost-cutting measures. Salaried workers were replaced by sharecroppers. Traditional crops that no longer commanded a good price at market were eliminated. Mosby mortgaged everything but the mansion in order to raise the capital to invest in equities. He reasoned that the value of stocks, which had plummeted after the Crash, eventually would have to rebound. When Emory went off to the University of Virginia, he recalled his father telling him that history was a good hobby, but he should concentrate on the study of commerce. "Ask your professors what stocks they would buy if they had any money," he instructed. Despite his father's urgings, however, Emory majored in history and graduated with honors just as the dark curtain of fascism descended over Europe.

The Second World War proved a boon for the Ashcrofts. Devon's bounty was sent down river to feed the shipbuilders in Newport News and the servicemen stationed around Hampton Roads. Emory's draft board agreed with his father that, as an only son whose father was engaged in "essential production," he could best serve his country by helping to see that the plantation ran smoothly. Emory set aside his plans to enlist and become a wartime correspondent, returned to Devon, and reluctantly began to learn the farming business from his father. Eventually he assumed responsibility for recruiting workers to operate the farm and servants to handle domestic chores. With young, able-bodied men serving in the military and women working on assembly lines, Emory's labor options were limited mostly to teenagers, old-timers, and disabled persons. Mosby was impressed with Emory's ability to locate individuals willing to undertake menial tasks, but ensuring that they actually put in a good day's work did not prove to be his son's strong suit. Mosby complained that he was the only living Ashcroft willing to "go out and kick ass" when jobs weren't getting done.

Weekends found the Ashcrofts entertaining high-ranking officers, defense contractors, and foreign dignitaries who happened to be in the vicinity of Hampton Roads. Rumors circulated that Devon hosted more than one secret meeting regarding war-time business. So active was the social life at Devon during the war that Emory had to hire a woman just to coordinate dinner parties and other functions. The person he found, a local girl with two years of college and a gift for entertaining, eventually became his wife. Emory referred to Gray Wagoner Ashcroft as his "salvation" and the "heart and soul" of Devon.

As Emory's family history drew closer to the present, I wondered what had gone so wrong that Mrs. Ashcroft worried about leaving her husband alone. She had alluded to financial problems, but plenty of people face such challenges and manage to live full and satisfying lives. Granted, I was not a psychiatrist, but I had cared for enough depressed patients to sense when someone was capable of harming himself or others. I had no such inkling about Emory. Quite the opposite, in fact. Here was a healthy, debonair, attractive man of fifty-seven blessed with a keen mind, a good memory, a passion for family history, and a magnificent wife who obviously cared deeply for him. I reflected on my own circumstances with more than a tinge of jealousy.

When Emory reached the end of his family history, he offered some perspective on the Ashcrofts' finances. Paying down the mortgages on refinanced sections of the plantation had been difficult. So, too, was finding decent farm labor. Too many job opportunities beckoned from fast-growing Hampton Roads and Richmond. Emory's father began to lose interest in plantation business after the war and shifted more and more responsibilities to Emory. At this point, Emory abruptly concluded his lecture, simply stating that he had studied to be a historian, not a farm manager. We returned to the library as shadows filled the unlit room and daylight gave way to gloaming. My host grew quiet.

Feeling that my visit had come to an end, I expressed my appreciation for the family history and turned to leave. For some reason, though, I stopped and added that such an illustrious past must be part legacy and part liability. Emory looked at me in a curious way, half-frightened and half-ready to retaliate, as if he'd just been grazed by a bullet. He quickly collected himself, though, and asked, "Do you have a family, Doctor Curry?" I realized that the query was Emory's way of maneuvering the conversation away from himself, and I also knew that he would be offended if I failed to reveal anything about myself. To understand this man, I first would need to gain his trust.

Emory refilled my glass as I took a seat and explained why I moved my practice from Richmond to Charles City County. He, of course, knew of my former in-laws and recalled that they had visited Devon on more than one occasion. I spoke of growing up

with the burden of being the first Curry to seek a college educa-
tion. Then I explained that my parents sacrificed greatly in order
to send me to the University of Virginia. Becoming a physician
was my way of thanking them for their efforts.

"In other words," Emory interjected, "you would have preferred taking a different direction."

"It's been too long ago," I responded. "Perhaps the choice I
made was the choice I was meant to make. Who knows?"

I felt strangely apologetic about the brevity of my account, as
if I had simply reviewed case notes in a medical file, not captured
the nuances of my life. There was little in the way of depth or
drama. Emory, to his credit, had listened politely, his expression
changing only once, and then just for a second when I mentioned
that my ex-wife and I fortunately had not had any children.

An awkward silence followed my remarks. Emory finally spoke,
in a voice free of affect. "I know why you're here, Russell."

Naturally I felt foolish for not being more forthcoming and
asked, "Do you think there's anything wrong with you?" I empha-
sized the first "you."

"I could be flip, but that would be unkind. It's rare to get a
house call these days. A direct question deserves a direct answer.
I may be suffering from a mild case of disappointment. Do they
teach you how to cure disappointment in medical school, Russell?"

"We learned how to recognize disappointment, not how to cure
it," I admitted.

Emory took a sip of bourbon and looked past me. "What's the
use of recognizing what we don't know how to cure? Under the
circumstances, wouldn't ignorance be preferable?"

The two of us now were sitting in almost total darkness. I asked
Emory if he would mind turning on a light. As he reached over
to the floor lamp beside his chair, I heard him mutter something
about the world needing less light and more insight.

"I'm just a country doc, not a psychiatrist," I pointed out, immediately embarrassed that I sounded like Sam Ervin at the Wa-
tergate hearings. "But I'd be glad to refer you to a colleague of
mine at MCV. He's an expert on depression."

"Did I say I was depressed, Russell? Richmond needs psychiatrists; I don't."

"I didn't mean to offend you," I responded, once again standing to take my leave.

"No offense taken. I'd be honored if you'd care to drop by for a bourbon now and then."

The invitation must have been Emory's way of telling me that he realized he could use some help. I was flattered that he felt comfortable in my company, and, quite frankly, I welcomed the opportunity to get to know him better. Bachelor living had its benefits, but after ten years the pangs of loneliness were starting to displace the pleasures of solitude.

As Emory escorted me from the library, I noticed several golf clubs sticking out of an umbrella stand. "I see you're a golfer."

A broad smile crossed Emory's face. "How else would I have learned to endure disappointment?"

"I understand completely," I added.

When we reached the door, I asked Emory to say goodbye to his wife for me and thanked him for the hospitality and history lesson. Just then the phone rang, and Emory excused himself to answer it, apologizing for not walking me out. As I strolled to my vehicle, I heard Mrs. Ashcroft's stage whisper from the front garden. "Doctor Curry, how'd it go with Emory?"

I explained that he had shared the history of the Ashcroft clan.

"Did he speak of his father?"

I told her what I could recall, mostly about how Mosby Ashcroft had revived Devon after the drought of 1930 and then gradually shifted responsibility for the plantation onto Emory's shoulders.

"He didn't mention his father's death?"

I shook my head.

"Well, Emory should have said something. There was speculation that Mosby took his own life. But no one could ever prove it."

"Did he have any reason why he might have wanted to kill himself?"

"You're looking at her," Gray softly answered.

Chapter 3

ANOTHER HOUSE CALL TO DEVON

I first visited Devon on April 13. I remember the date for two reasons. April 13 is Thomas Jefferson's birthday, a day that I regard with the same reverence that Christians reserve for December 25. April 13 also is two days before the day when loyal citizens of Mr. Jefferson's democracy annually offer up their tithe to sustain his noble experiment. The day after my visit to Devon was spent with my accountant, putting the finishing touches on my tax forms. Whenever I confront this annual ritual, I must remind myself that I did not become a physician in order to make a fortune. To be honest, I'm not at all sure why I continued practicing medicine after my divorce. Lack of imagination, I suppose. In any event, I had intended to call on Emory the next day, April 15, but just as I was leaving the office, I received a call from Branch Pruitt. His wife's water broke and she had no intention of delivering anywhere but her own home.

The next day, April 16, I closed the office at 4:00 p.m. and drove to Devon. Gray, who by this time had departed for the pagan playground of California, suggested that I not call first, but simply drop by. Something about Emory refusing to answer the phone when he was immersed in one of his innumerable projects. Apparently he also avoided phone calls when he felt reclusive, which Gray said was becoming more common. Then there was

Edward, the elderly African American who helped out around the mansion. He was almost completely deaf and unable to hear the phone ring. Since Emory's hearing wasn't all that good to begin with, Gray pestered him to purchase one of those phones that lights up when there's an incoming call, but he would have none of it. His standard retort was, "If I spent as much time on the phone as other folks, I'd be just as ill-informed. Man's got to have time to himself if he ever hopes to court wisdom."

Driving east along Route 5, I thought about Gray's concern for Emory's mental health and indulged in a little self-pity, my own circumstances being such that no one gave a comparable damn for my well-being. In any event, I had little reason, based on my first meeting with Emory, to share Gray's level of concern for her husband. He struck me as a man in quiet control of his life; someone who possessed a clear sense of who he was. What's more, he liked being who he was. Discontent being the basic state of human nature, not many men could make a similar claim. The more I reflected on Emory, in fact, the more I believed he would be one of the last people I would expect to do something rash or self-destructive.

After parking my Jeep in Devon's driveway, I hesitated before getting out. How, I wondered, could I learn more about Gray's disturbing disclosure several days earlier? Would I offend Emory or betray a confidence if I inquired about the circumstances surrounding his father's death? I decided it was better to wait until Tobias returned from his golf junket. He likely would know whether Mosby Ashcroft committed suicide. Perhaps he also could shed light on Gray Ashcroft's odd remark as I was leaving.

Jeb met me as I stepped out of the Jeep, sniffed a few times, and returned to his post on the front steps. I knocked on the door repeatedly, but no one answered. A quick reconnaissance revealed no sign of activity: no lights on in the mansion, no Edward around, no sounds of farm machinery. Maybe Emory decided to accompany his wife on her trip. As I headed back to the Jeep, however, I detected a faint sound like the popping of a distant Champagne cork. Then nothing. Opening the Jeep's door, I heard the sound again. Then nothing. I waited a moment and, sure as sin, the popping sound repeated. It seemed to come from the immense lawn that gently sloped from the mansion down to the River. A hedge of tall boxwoods obscured my view, so I went to have a better look. What I saw made me smile. There was Emory, halfway down the lawn, clad in Bermuda shorts, an orange polo shirt, and black socks, driving golf balls into the James.

I watched him for several minutes, then applauded when he sent one ball a good two hundred yards on a bead. Emory turned, his surprise quickly passing as he recognized his audience of one. "I highly recommend this therapy, Doc. It's a surefire cure for perplexity."

"I didn't realize perplexity was an illness. Besides, to my way of thinking, there's nothing more perplexing than the game of golf."

"Point well made," Emory replied as he strolled up the lawn to shake my hand. "I'm glad to see you, Russell. Care to join me?"

Flattered that my unannounced visit had not been seen as an unwanted intrusion, I accepted Emory's offer. For the next hour, we punctuated drives with unsolicited golf tips and banter about the pains and pleasures of the game. My original reason for dropping by was all but forgotten as I eased into the casual company of a fellow man, a diversion to which I had not been treated in a long time. While I enjoyed my partnership with Tobias, the relationship was more avuncular than fraternal. When we did manage to work in a round of golf, which was infrequent, the conversation invariably turned to business and his impending retirement. He would start running down the list of his patients, explaining their family histories, quirks, bad habits, and probable causes of eventual death. My partner seemed to derive some macabre satisfaction from accurately predicting how his patients would die. I once asked him if he also took the necessary steps to make certain his predictions came true. Tobias was not amused. Had he made a guess, I wondered, about how Emory Ashcroft would meet his maker?

When Emory and I had emptied his bucket of used golf balls, he suggested we repair to the patio for a bourbon. As he disappeared into the mansion, I debated whether to risk spoiling an enjoyable interlude by inquiring about his health. If Tobias were back from North Carolina, I would have been tempted to return Emory to my partner's care so I simply could take advantage of his companionship. Since meeting Emory and Gray, my appetite for getting to know them better had grown. Normally I maintained a respectable distance between myself and the people around me, but something told me that these two charming individuals might play an important role in my life. What that role would be, however, remained as unclear as the morning fog along the James.

Emerging from the mansion, Emory called out, "Edward will be here presently with our reward."

"Exactly what have we done to earn a reward?" I asked.

"Our barrage of golf balls prevented the Yankee gunboats from advancing on Richmond," Emory replied with a chuckle as he sank heavily into a lawn chair.

In a few minutes Edward appeared with a silver tray containing two glasses, a small ice bucket, and a decanter of bourbon. Emory took the tray, placed it on the table between us, and introduced Edward. "Doctor Curry, I'd like you to meet Devon's oldest and finest resident, Edward Washington. Most folks in these parts refer to Edward as the Professor."

Nodding to Edward, I asked Emory, "How'd he come by that name?" Edward surprised me by responding, "It's my years, Doctor Curry. I guess people think some kind of wisdom attaches itself to age."

Embarrassed that I hadn't directed my question to Edward, I apologized and explained that I was told he was hard of hearing.

Edward looked around as if he had not heard a word I said. Emory asked him if he'd care to join us for a drink, but he shook his head and slowly walked back to the mansion.

"He hears when he wants to and what he wants to," Emory confided. "I'm never quite sure what he picks up."

Intrigued, I asked Emory how long had the Professor worked at Devon. Emory said his father hired Edward before he was born.

"That's over half a century!" I said in amazement. "I'll bet he could tell some stories."

"Indeed he could, my friend, but he never would, at least not to strangers. Edward's the most loyal person I know when it comes to this plantation and the Ashcrofts. I don't fully understand why, but I suspect it goes back a long way. I don't think Edward ever got over Dad's passing."

Sensing an opportunity to follow up on Gray's comment about Mosby Ashcroft's death, I considered asking Emory about it, but decided instead to ask what Emory meant earlier when he spoke of perplexity. To this day I can see Emory draining the last of his bourbon and gazing out at the River, seemingly weighing whether or not to respond to my query. After a moment or two, he turned back toward me and softly replied, "I still don't know you very well, Russell, but you strike me as an honorable man and a member of an honorable profession. If I answer your question, I would like to know that it doesn't leave these premises."

I told Emory a physician was duty-bound to keep any and all patient information confidential.

Emory looked me square in the eyes. "I'm asking you as a friend, not as a doctor."

After receiving my assurance that his remarks would be held in the strictest confidence, Emory recounted what he called "Devon's retreat from prosperity." He repeated what he told me during my first visit about his father's decision to mortgage portions of the plantation to finance the purchase of equities, then explained that most of this money had been invested in railroad stocks. Mosby Ashcroft's investments fared reasonably well during the war, but afterwards they took a hit as the commercial trucking industry expanded and passenger travel by train gave way to the automobile. Dividends dwindled, and the value of the Ashcroft portfolio dropped.

During this troubling time, Emory assumed greater responsibility for Devon's management. He felt growing pressure to boost farm production in order to pay down his father's debts. No longer blessed with time to indulge his passion for local history, Emory devoted most of his time to learning about crop yields, soil conditions, weather forecasts, and commodity markets. For a time, it appeared his efforts were achieving a measure of financial stability, but Emory was quick to point out that stability simply meant the Ashcrofts weren't falling deeper in debt. Then the bottom fell out.

Emory likened what happened in the early seventies to the plagues visited upon Egypt. First came problems finding labor, as an increasing number of local able-bodied males sought higher wages and greater job security in the factories and warehouses of Richmond. Then came the flooding of the James in 1972 and the inundation of over a third of Devon's fields. According to Emory, the River was so full of toxic material from the factories around Hopewell that he feared nothing of value would be grown ever again on the land covered by flood waters.

Ultimately, however, the worst of the "plagues" was double-digit inflation. As farm production costs skyrocketed, Emory found that he could not afford to cultivate additional acreage. Interest rates rose to prohibitive heights, depriving Devon of the capital needed to purchase more efficient machinery and thereby offset the loss of farm hands. The last straw was the shutdown of the North Carolina plant that provided fertilizer for Devon's fields. Thanks to a shortage of natural gas, the plant was unable to produce the nitrogen so essential to farming in the Piedmont. Emory told me that the previous year's income from the plantation's agricultural operations rose 14 percent, which sounded impressive except for the fact that production costs jumped 20 percent. As Emory continued explaining the hard times that befell Devon, I couldn't help wondering whether my own practice eventually would suffer as my patients found it harder to cover the rising costs of medical care and insurance.

When my host was done, I said, "You're worried that you might have to give up Devon, aren't you?"

"Worried? Hell yes, I'm worried. I can't stop worrying."

I hadn't expected so visceral a response.

"I'm also disappointed, disappointed that I couldn't make a go of it, disappointed that the soil containing the remains of my ancestors might be abandoned, disappointed that the final pathetic chapter of a great Virginia clan had to be written on my watch." Emory paused momentarily to pour himself more bourbon, neglecting to offer me a refill. "Every member of my family has made a contribution to this place. When it was necessary, they worked in the fields alongside the farm hands. They took care of their own sick, raised their own food, spun their own cloth, delivered their own babies. My father looked after his workers long after they were too old to put in a day's work. My mother sold her jewelry so Dad could buy a new tractor. What contributions have I made? What'll Gray put on my gravestone? If things keep going the way they're going, of course, she won't be able to afford a gravestone."

As he told me of his concerns, Emory's eyes never left mine, his hands tightened their grip on the arms of his chair, and the color rose in his cheeks. Finally, he appeared to relax a bit and his voice softened. "Let me tell you, Russell, disappointment is like a riptide. The more you resist it, the weaker you get."

Searching for something constructive to say, I mustered a half-hearted reply. "Surely there's some alternative to losing Devon." I was beginning to understand why Gray was so concerned for her husband's welfare.

Emory turned away and offered no response to my question.

"You haven't put Devon up for sale yet, have you?"

"No, sir. I'm not sure I could bring myself to do that. Probably have to kill myself before I'd sell Devon. But we did get an offer."

"An offer for Devon?" I repeated. "From whom?"

"Don't know. That's the God's honest truth. The offer was tendered by the buyer's lawyer. Apparently the buyer wished to remain anonymous."

"Was it a good offer?" I asked without thinking.

"What does it matter? I cannot afford to maintain Devon, and I cannot bring myself to sell it."

I realized that Emory felt completely immobilized by the circumstances facing him. A desperate man with options is a danger to those around him. A desperate man with no options is a danger to himself. Emory clearly believed he had run out of options.

"Do you know why my wife went to California, despite the fact she's scared to death of flying?"

I shook my head.

"She's out there trying to convince her daughter's husband to buy Devon, so we can keep the place somewhat in the family."

"Somewhat?"

Emory explained that he and Gray had no children of their own, but she had a daughter with her first husband. Carol Ann lived at Devon through her adolescence, and Emory had been devoted to her, but she and her mother argued constantly. When she left home to attend Yale, Carol Ann told Emory that she loved him dearly, but he should not expect her to return to Devon after college. Following graduation, Carol Ann "squandered" – Gray's term—a year traveling around the United States with a young man she insisted was just a friend. Eventually she decided to settle in Los Angeles and work in a private psychiatric facility for well-to-do women. She fell in love with and married the brother of one of her patients, an entrepreneur from a prominent family. Brad, Carol Ann's husband, was worth a fortune, and Gray hoped he would have no problem purchasing Devon if he so desired.

The hour was getting late, but Emory requested that I accompany him on his nightly stroll around the grounds. As he continued discussing the dilemma facing him, I wondered what would happen if Brad declined to buy Devon. Without other heirs, the property would be sold at some point, so why turn down a good offer now? I shared my thought with Emory.

"Russell, your point is perfectly understandable." There wasn't a trace of annoyance in Emory's voice. "What I haven't told you is that Gray and I hoped to set up a trust so that after we are gone Devon will be preserved as you now see it. We envisioned a place with a historian-in-residence, a place where school children could learn what plantation life was really like."

"Slavery included?" I asked.

"Of course," Emory responded, sounding offended. "It's important for young people to know how these great plantations were built and maintained. Too often in these parts they get an overly romanticized version of the old days. Gray and I actually hired an architect to draw up a plan for converting the stables into a dormitory so children could stay overnight."

"What a laudable idea!" Getting to know Emory was like driving for the first time on a picturesque country road. Pleasant surprises just kept popping up.

"My biggest nightmare," Emory continued, "is that some Yankee developer will get his hands on Devon and turn it into one of those God-awful gated golf communities. My ancestors gave their sweat and blood for this place. They deserve better."

We walked in silence for the next few minutes, providing an opportunity for me to fall further under Devon's spell. My senses were treated to the pungent smell of boxwoods and the serenading of frogs and crickets, while my mind drifted back in time. If history is holy, we were treading on sacred soil. I imagined what it must have been like to be master of Devon before the Revolutionary War and during McClellan's occupation. Emory began to point out places of significance around the grounds. Over in a grove west of the formal gardens his great grandmother had ordered her servants to hang burlap bags of family silver, liquor, and hams in the trees to hide them from Union soldiers. Behind the old ice house were the ruins of the world's second oldest bourbon distillery. Only Berkeley's distillery predated it. Emory smiled when I volunteered to erect a monument to mark the spot.

Eventually we entered the formal gardens directly behind the mansion. Emory explained that Ashcroft women insisted on fresh flowers on the entry and dining tables. To prevent deer from devouring Devon's flowers, boxwoods had been planted close together to form a natural barrier. Apparently the bushes' distinctive odor repelled the rapacious herbivores.

At the far end of the furthest garden from the mansion, sheltered in an alcove cut into the boxwood hedge, I noticed an odd-shaped object. At a distance in the dimming light it looked like an upended birdbath. When I inquired, Emory informed me that my initial impression was accurate. The object was indeed a birdbath that had been turned over, pedestal-end up, by the first Emory Allen Ashcroft. I sensed another family story would be forthcoming.

It seems that Emory's great grandfather was devoted to his only daughter, Abigail. The young girl loved to watch the birds that fluttered around the plantation, so her father commissioned a Richmond stonemason to create an ornate birdbath for her tenth birthday. Abigail spent hours in the garden watching robins, sparrows, and finches cavorting as they quenched their thirst in the birdbath.

When General McClellan commandeered Devon and converted it to a field hospital during the Peninsula Campaign, the Ashcrofts were allowed to remain in their quarters on the second floor. Emory explained that this unusually generous arrangement caused some neighbors to suspect that his great grandfather had either cut a deal with McClellan or that he actually was a Union sympathizer. In any event, Abigail, who by this time was in her late teens, began helping out in the field hospital, which was how she met a young Union soldier from Massachusetts. He had been severely wounded at Seven Pines and probably would have died had it not been for Abigail's nursing.

After the war, the young man returned to Devon to ask for Abigail's hand in marriage. Her father adamantly refused to endorse the union for reasons that were never clear. Some relatives thought that giving his blessing to Abigail and the young man would have confirmed neighbors' suspicions that the old man's blood ran blue, not gray. Others guessed that his refusal was prompted by an unnatural desire to keep his beloved daughter close. Unable to secure her father's blessing, Abigail eloped, whereupon the distraught patriarch disowned her and ordered that her name never again be spoken in his presence. In a final symbolic act, he had Abigail's birdbath turned upside down. It was even rumored that he took to shooting the birds Abigail had loved so much to watch.

As Emory related this sad tale, I couldn't help being struck by how engaged and animated he had become. Sharing stories about his family appeared to be an effective therapy for my host. I hoped, though, that he would not ask about my own roots, since my woeful lack of knowledge regarding my ancestors made me self-conscious and somewhat embarrassed in his presence.

Walking back to the mansion, Emory offered me a nightcap and a cigar, explaining that the only time he could enjoy the pleasures of tobacco was when Gray was away. I accepted the drink, but declined the cigar. I did, however, resist the temptation to preach about the dangers of smoking. Emory left me in the library while he went to fetch the brandy. Since my first visit, the library's tables and chairs had become littered with assorted files and pieces of paper.

When Emory returned with two snifters and a decanter, he noticed that I was surveying his "droppings" and explained that he was working on a history of Charles City County cemeteries. He expressed a sense of urgency about the project because a number of old burial grounds had been abandoned, their gravestones either vandalized or weathered beyond recognition. The thought of an inscription becoming illegible before it could be recorded for posterity upset Emory. "We must never lose track of those who preceded us," he proclaimed as he drained the contents of his glass.

Pouring himself another brandy, Emory began to relate fascinating stories about local graveyards. One involved the second wife of a prominent lawyer who demanded that his first wife's casket be dug up and moved so that her own casket, when the time came, would separate her husband's casket from his first wife's mortal remains. Emory quipped that the woman had no intention of allowing her husband's first marriage to be rekindled in eternity. Another story concerned a man who worried that his family burial plot was located too close to the James River. The water table in Charles City County is pretty high, and he apparently feared that a heavy rain might cause the ground to give up its dead. The man ordered that his casket be placed in a bateau when he died and that both be buried in the family plot. If a flood did occur, he figured he could ride it out.

Jeb started scratching at the front door, so Emory let him out to pee and picked up where he left off. Several years earlier folks visiting one of the local cemeteries noticed that rocks had been piled up on a particular grave. When Emory heard about it, he assumed the deceased had been Jewish, as it was their custom to place rocks instead of flowers on graves. Rocks last longer, as they say. Emory went to take a look, and sure enough, there was a collection of good-sized rocks on the burial mound. The grave-stone indicated that the dead man's name was McGinnis, clearly not a Jewish name. Sometime later, Emory learned that McGinnis' former business partner and later rival was responsible for the rock pile, apparently an attempt to ensure that McGinnis never rose from the dead.

I couldn't stop laughing as Emory spun one odd tale after an-other. On several occasions laughter led to tears, and I told my host he would make a great comedian. As one who dealt with death on a regular basis, I never fully appreciated its humorous side until that evening with Emory.

Following another refill, Emory turned to one of his latest interests, African American cemeteries. According to him, no ef-fort had been made to inventory the numerous African American burial sites in Charles City County. Some of the sites predated the Civil War and were no longer maintained. Emory explained that after Reconstruction vengeful whites had torched several black churches, compelling congregations to re-locate and leave their deceased relatives behind. In other cases, black families moved to Tidewater cities or Richmond in search of work and left their family plots to be reclaimed by the weeds and brambles.

Listening to Emory, I realized that the man would love nothing more than to spend his days recording the history of his native land. What a loss it would be, I thought at the time, if something were to happen that prevented him from pursuing his calling. I also recall feeling slightly jealous that my host possessed a true passion. Medical practice no longer provided the spark it once did for me. There were too many high-priced specialists corner-ing the market on the most interesting cases. Docs like me were left to handle the routine stuff.

Emory was in the midst of telling me about poor folks during the Great Depression who "borrowed" the unoccupied burial plots of their neighbors so they could give their loved ones a final resting place when I realized that several snifters of brandy had gone to my head, creating a not unpleasant buzz, but causing me to worry about negotiating the country roads in the dark. I thanked Emory for a most entertaining evening, patted Jeb, and walked to my Jeep. Emory followed and cautioned me to keep an eye out for deer on the way home. I was about to climb in the driver's seat when Emory stopped me.

"I know you're around death all the time, Russell," he stated, "but do you ever wonder how you're likely to die?"

The question struck me as odd at first, but then I realized that we had just spent the past hour talking about cemeteries and burials.

"Of course I do," I replied. "It's only natural as we grow older to wonder how we're going to go."

"That's just it, my friend. I don't."

Chapter 4

MEDICAL RECORDS: OFFICIAL AND UNOFFICIAL

Maybe it was the bourbon and the brandy nightcap, but after leaving Devon I decided to drop by the office on the way back home. It occurred to me that Tobias probably had been Mosby Ashcroft's physician toward the end of his life and that his medical records might contain information on the old man's cause of death. I wasn't quite sure why it mattered so much to me, but I suspected it had more to do with Gray Ashcroft than Emory.

When I joined Tobias' practice, he insisted that we maintain separate medical records. I surmised at the time that his patient notes were pretty informal and that he might be embarrassed if I had access to them. Any time I needed to check on one of his patients, he always reviewed the file in private and related the contents to me verbally.

I located Tobias' files behind the ancient desk in his office and pulled out the drawer marked A-E. There were thick files for Azure Cabell Ashcroft, Mosby's wife, and Gray Wagoner Ashcroft, and thinner files for Mosby Martin Ashcroft, Jr. and Emory Allen Ashcroft, Mosby Senior's two sons. There was no file, however, for their father, Mosby Martin Ashcroft. I searched the entire drawer, then the contents of the other drawers, thinking Mosby's records might have been misplaced, but I could not find them anywhere. It was inconceivable that Tobias had treated all the Ashcrofts except Mosby. The patriarch's missing file only heightened my curiosity regarding Gray's cryptic remark concerning his death. I was tempted to examine Gray's records, but I decided against it for reasons that had nothing to do with medical ethics. Besides the hour was late and I was getting sleepy.

Tobias was due back from his golfing junket the next day, and I planned to ask him about Mosby Ashcroft. My partner typically arrived at the office by 7:00 a.m. and ate a light breakfast before seeing his first patient. Grace Diamond, our receptionist, always had coffee and a bran muffin waiting for Tobias. I normally came to the office just in time for my first appointment, which Grace usually scheduled for 8:30 a.m., but that morning I showed up as Grace was getting out of her car. She took one look at me and asked if I'd been in a bar fight. I requested coffee when it was ready and took a seat in Tobias' office. A few minutes later he walked in the front door, greeted Grace, and entered his office.

"I know something's wrong," Tobias grumbled when he saw me, "if you're at work before me."

Setting aside the usual pleasantries and inquiries about his golf game, I blurted out the question that was on my mind. "What can you tell me about the death of Mosby Ashcroft?"

Startled, Tobias gave me a professorial stare that silently implied impertinent inquisitiveness. You would have thought I asked him if any of his ancestors had fought in the Union army.

I apologized for catching him off guard and explained Gray's phone call and my visits to Devon.

Tobias shut the door to his office and sat down. "I'm not surprised by Gray's concern," he said. "Emory's been under enormous pressure for some time now. Between the flood, the creditors, and the insurance investigators, he's had a lot to deal with."

"Emory never mentioned insurance investigators," I replied. "Were they looking into Mosby's death?"

Tobias lit his pipe, taking several short drags to get a slow burn going. "The insurance men were convinced that old Mosby had purposely taken his life."

"What was the official cause of death?"

"Drowning."

"Why did the investigators think it was suicide? Did he leave a note?"

"No, there was no note, but Mosby spent his entire life on the River. He knew what to do and what not to do around water. It was Emory that discovered Mosby's body washed ashore a little downstream from Devon's dock. As far as we could determine, he had drunk heavily the night before, put on a heavy overcoat, and taken his boat out."

"So he fell overboard and was unable to save himself?" I conjectured.

"That's the story the family insisted on," Tobias responded. "But no one could figure out why he put on a heavy wool overcoat. It was July!"

"Where does Gray fit into all this?"

Tobias gave me a knowing look. "She is striking, isn't she?"

I made no reply, but I could feel my face redden.

"Emory married Gray in 1962, as I recall. Same year JFK blockaded Cuba. They wanted to have children and tried for more than a year. They even came to me for help. In the midst of all this, Emory's mother suffered a stroke and was partially paralyzed. Mosby believed that Azure had only a little time left, and he was absolutely convinced that she could not pass in peace without knowing that a grandchild had been born to carry on the Ashcroft blood line. I suspect Mosby, who was as forceful a person as you'd ever care to meet, put a lot of pressure on Gray and Emory to produce an heir."

"Not exactly a prescription for productive sex," I pointed out.

"No indeed. It's a wonder Gray and Emory didn't cut and run. I certainly would have."

"Do you think Mosby took his life because his wife was dying and he had no grandchild?"

Grace knocked on the door. "Sorry to interrupt, but I brought you both a cinnamon bun and coffee. God knows, Doctor Curry needs it."

When Grace left, Tobias continued. "I wasn't only Mosby's physician, Russell. I was a close friend. Truth be told, though, I never really understood the man. He'd give you the shirt off his back.

I've never known such generosity. He rarely asked for anything, but when he did make a request, he expected it to be honored. No, he insisted that it be honored. I remember once during the war he asked me to be on call for several days. Some top secret meeting of bigwigs was going to be held at Devon, and he had been asked to make sure a physician was available. I agreed, of course, but I also explained that I had other patients to take care of. I gave him the phone numbers of two colleagues in Richmond who could back me up in an emergency. Wouldn't you know that the one time I was needed at Devon I had to be over at the Shifletts tending to the grandmother. Mosby was infuriated and refused to have anything to do with me for months."

Tobias went on to explain that Mosby pressured both Gray and Emory to get tested to see if either of them was incapable of having children. The tests indicated that Gray was unable to carry another baby to term. Two days later Mosby's body was found. I wondered about the effect it must have had on Emory to find his father's body. Tobias was certain Emory blamed himself for Mosby's death. Once again I had gotten information that supported Gray's concern for her husband's mental health.

Tobias told me in strictest confidence that he had been placed in a very awkward position with regard to Mosby's death. Mosby's life insurance policy would have been nullified if he had committed suicide. Two investigators from the insurance company deposed Tobias and appropriated Mosby's medical records. The fact that Tobias' records were not very thorough or legible doubtless made the case for suicide more difficult to prove. The investigators wanted to know about Mosby's mental condition, drinking habits, financial situation, and family relations. At one point they asked Tobias point blank whether he believed Mosby was capable of taking his own life. Tobias told me he evaded the question by asking the investigators if they thought a drunk driver who ran off the road and hit a tree necessarily should be considered suicidal.

I was interested to know how the matter of Mosby's life insurance finally was resolved. Tobias said he had heard that several of Mosby's influential friends in Richmond pressured the insurance company to settle rather than go to court. "My official judgment," Tobias stressed the word official, "was that Mosby's death was due to accidental causes. He had been drinking heavily. No note was ever found. Who was I to second guess the man?"

I thanked Tobias for filling me in and started to leave, but something told me he had something else to say.

"To me," he continued, "the oddest thing about the whole affair was Mosby's body washing ashore just yards down river from the dock. You could dump a hundred bodies into the James and ninety-nine of them would be carried miles downstream. The currents in these parts can be pretty strong. Searchers actually found Mosby's boat near Jamestown Island. Folks around here said Mosby couldn't escape Devon, even in death."

We chatted a few minutes longer about the Ashcrofts and what it must be like to be born into Virginia aristocracy. Like myself, Tobias' origins were more modest, and he, too, shared my fascination with people of privilege and power. Tobias commented on Gray's marriage to Emory and noted that her "roots rested in even shallower soil than our own." Apparently Gray's father had been a tenant farmer at Devon. She grew up in awe of life in the "big house," even played games with her young friends where she pretended to be the mistress of Devon. As she grew into a lovely young woman, some folks accused her of putting on airs. It was bad enough to be rich and act that way, they said, but to be poor and do so was vexing. Then Gray got pregnant and people said her unfortunate circumstances were a proper punishment for thinking she was more than she was.

My desire to learn more about Gray and the Ashcroft clan was stoked, but I expected my first patient in a few minutes. I had one more question, though, that needed to be answered.

"Tobias, now that you're back, you'll be seeing Emory if he needs medical care. Are you worried about him?"

To this day I remember exactly what he said. "You're a Cavaliers' fan, aren't you?"

"If you mean the University of Virginia football team, the answer is yes, but what's that got to do with Emory?"

"You know, I suspect, how it feels to attend games in Charlottesville and watch the Cavaliers cling to a narrow lead. Loyalty and that old narcotic, hope, keep you watching, but you already understand that the final outcome will be another loss. The opposing team will rally in the waning minutes of the game and eke out a victory. It's as if the game's been scripted. Knowing this in advance, however, is no help. You won't leave the game early. You'll still get excited, cheer loudly, allow your hopes to swell, and then watch helplessly as another win eludes the orange and blue. What I've just described is how it is with Emory, I believe. He knows what the final outcome will be for Devon, but he can't bring himself to accept it and move on."

"So you think Emory will go on hoping Devon can be saved, even though in the end he'll be forced to sell?"

"Yes, sir, that's my clinical judgment."

"Do you worry that Emory might take his own life?"

"Not for a second," Tobias replied as he knocked the ashes from his pipe. "Killing yourself requires ambition and drive. It's not in Emory's nature to take the initiative. He'll hang on to Devon until his creditors demand that the sheriff evict him. By refusing to sell, he at least can say that Devon was taken from him, against his will."

"Isn't there a fine line between selling your place and having it seized by creditors?"

Just then Grace knocked on the door and announced that Tobias' first appointment had arrived. "I suspect Emory has lived most of his life along that fine line, Russell." As I stood to leave, Tobias grabbed my elbow and muttered under his breath, "I'm pleased you're concerned about Emory. He's a gentleman and a scholar, and he could use a friend, one who doesn't know him as well as I do."

I wanted to ask Tobias what he meant, but Grace was ushering in Mrs. Southall. My partner may have felt confident that Emory would not harm himself, but I was less certain. I decided to keep in touch with Emory. There was something pure and honest about the man, qualities that appealed to me and made me feel protective toward him. Gray was due back from Los Angeles the next day, Friday. I decided to drop by on Saturday afternoon and find out how financial negotiations had gone with Gray's daughter and her husband.

On Saturday I was preparing to leave the office around 1:30 p.m. when Grace rushed in. As far as I knew no patients remained in the waiting room, so I thought it odd when Grace whispered, "Doctor Curry, you're not done yet." After catching her breath, she continued, "Rita Crockett's just arrived without an appointment, and she's got Red Buchanan with her. I know you were fixing to get out of here, but is there any way you can see them before you leave? Red doesn't look very good."

Grace was one of those people who would have made a terrific fund-raiser for an outfit like the March of Dimes. Her requests were harder to refuse than Smithfield ham biscuits. She was a large woman with an even bigger heart, and there wasn't a soul in Charles City County who wouldn't have given her their last dollar. I suspect one reason Grace struggled with her weight was all the tins of home-baked cookies and boxes of chocolates patients brought her when they showed up for appointments.

I agreed to see Rita and Red, prompting Grace to give me one of her patented smiles, the kind that could make a serial killer feel worthy. Instead of returning to the reception area, however, she shifted her weight from one foot to the other and looked around my office. This behavior, I had learned, meant Grace possessed some additional information that she was just itching to share, if only I would ask. Knowing her as I did, she probably figured if a person asked her what she was thinking, then sharing her thoughts was not gossiping. Grace was very critical of folks who gossiped about their neighbors. Over the years, thanks to her wealth of local knowledge and my willingness to play her game and initiate requests for details, I often was able to abbreviate the time-consuming chore of extracting patient histories.

"Is there anything else I should know, Grace?"

She beamed and proceeded to tell me that Red no longer could drive and that Rita regularly looked in on him to drop off groceries and make sure he was doing okay. I had seen Red several years earlier to stitch up a gash in his arm, so I was aware that Rachel, his wife, had died and that he lived with his son, Lee. Grace now informed me that Lee and Rita had been sweet on each other, but they never seemed quite ready to take the final step. Recently Lee had up and left. Grace was unsure why.

"If it weren't for Rita," Grace added, "I don't know what Red would do. She's a saint. Too bad his son's so worthless."

I sensed that Grace was getting warmed up for a discourse on ungrateful children, so I gently placed my hands on her shoulders and turned her toward the reception area. In a few moments she returned with Rita. Although I had never been formally introduced to Rita, I recognized her from the previous year's Fourth of July picnic. She was almost as tall as I was, with broad shoulders and a trim figure. I recalled seeing her because she was one of the few local women around my age who wasn't overweight or depressingly thin. She wore wire-rimmed glasses that made her look like a schoolteacher, and her auburn hair was pulled back in a girlish ponytail. In the parlance of the times, Rita was a real looker. I wondered why things between Red's son and her hadn't worked out.

"Doc, thanks so much for seeing us on short notice. Actually on no notice. Grace told me you were just about to leave." Rita paused briefly, her demeanor growing serious. "I'm worried about Red. He's sick, real sick. I bring him food, but he won't touch it. Says he's lost his appetite. You'll see when you look at him."

I asked Rita if there was anything more I should know before I examined Red.

She thought for a moment. "Did you know he's all alone now?"

I nodded. "Grace told me that Lee had left recently." Then for some foolish reason, I added, "That must have been tough on both of you."

Rita blushed, and tears started to well up in her eyes. "You don't know the half of it, Doc. Why is it that some men are so restless, even when everything they possibly could want is right in their own backyard?"

Though I didn't share my answer to Rita's question, I thought to myself, it's because having everything you desire is pretty damn scary. Men aren't prepared for it. They need to fight for something.

"Oh! One more thing," Rita said, lowering her voice. "No offense, but Red did not want to come here today. I had to make him do it for me."

"So I shouldn't expect him to be cooperative, is that it?"

Rita smiled warmly, "You must have been reading my mind, Doc."

Grace escorted Rita back to the waiting room and returned with Red. She kept trying to help him by placing her hand under his elbow, and he kept muttering that he wasn't dead yet. One look at Red, however, told me he was darn close. His gaunt figure and sallow coloring reminded me of a Confederate soldier I had seen in a movie years before. Rather than risk capture by a Yankee search party, he had run off into a Georgia swamp. He survived as best he could by killing small creatures with his bare hands and eating them raw. Red looked exactly like the soldier when he finally emerged from the swamp. He was no more than the shadow of the man I once had treated. If he weighed a 120 pounds, I'd have been surprised. His efforts to prop himself up on two canes clearly was a struggle. I pulled up a chair and motioned for Red to take a seat, but he grunted that he'd just as soon stand because he wasn't expecting to stay very long.

Red was one of the back country patients that Tobias had gladly transferred to me soon after I joined his practice. It wasn't that Red was an unpleasant sort, though I heard he could get pretty nasty when he drank too much. What made Red such a challenge was the man's mule-like stubbornness. Health warnings were as important to him as tango lessons. You could tell him about the dangers of nicotine or too much exposure to the sun, and he'd look you straight in the eye and tell you that we all have to die of something. "A man has a right to choose his executioner" was how he put it.

The one time I treated Red was a few months after moving to Charles City County. His wife, Rachel, dragged him to the office to show me a dark mole on his right arm. She had some experience as an LPN and realized that a mole that changed shape could be malignant. Sure enough, the mole proved to be cancerous. Rachel literally begged her husband to go to Richmond and have it removed.

I asked Red how he was feeling. He raised his head with difficulty so he could look me squarely in the eye. "How do I look, Doc?"

"You're not going to win any beauty contests," I responded.

Red managed a feeble chuckle. "That's for damn sure."

I asked Red to describe how he felt, and he replied that he had no energy to do things anymore. Couldn't even feed his hunting dogs. Rita had to do it. He added that his appetite was gone.

"Has anything happened that might have caused these problems?"

"Beats the hell out of me, Doc. All I know is life hasn't been worth living since Rachel passed."

"How about your son?"

Red started to turn around. "I'd best be going, Doc. I've taken enough of your time."

I moved so that I was standing between Red and the door and

explained that Grace told me about his son leaving.

Red mustered a look of total resignation. "That boy's an open wound, Doc. I intended to turn my place over to him when I joined Rachel. He could have made a decent living right here where he was born and raised. What's more, he couldn't have found a better woman than Rita. It's just like him to turn his back on a sure thing. Rachel, God rest her soul, hadn't been gone a year when we had a big blow-up."

I motioned once more for Red to take a seat, and this time he did. He informed me that his son resented being told who he should marry. When Red told Lee that his mother's dying wish was for him to settle down with Rita and start a family, Lee blew his stack, calling Red a hypocrite and accusing him of having devoted more time to his hunting dogs and his fishing than his wife when she was alive. Father and son traded below-the-belt insults until Lee finally declared that he wanted nothing more to do with his father and stormed off. The next day Rita heard from a local gas station attendant that Lee was heading south.

Having never had children of my own, advice about how to cope with a son's estrangement eluded me. I focused instead on learning more about Red's physical condition. He told me that breathing was difficult and his sleep fitful. Sometimes he experienced strange sensations like something was squeezing his insides. When I asked him to point to where he felt these sensations, he placed a forefinger on his chest and then moved it under his right arm.

I asked Red if he minded having a brief physical exam, and he managed to quip that it was okay as long as a reasonably attractive nurse did the examining. The fact that he had not lost his sense of humor was an encouraging sign, but my initial assessment remained grim. As I helped Red remove his shirt, we engaged in what Grace would call "man talk." Red asked me if I had tried any of the fishing holes he told me about when I saw him for his skin cancer. I admitted that I had been too busy to do any fishing. Red looked at me for a moment, then advised me not to put off the important things in life.

"Like fishing?" I responded.

Red acknowledged that his dream had long been to become a fishing guide. Bricklaying was all right for earning a living, but it didn't do much for the soul. I wanted to ask him what fishing did for his soul, but I started to choke up at the thought that this decent man, this man who had tried as best he knew to be a good husband and father, would never realize his life-long dream. Normally I avoided such an emotional reaction to my patients' problems. Detached concern was a physician's mantra. But Red's case, I suspect, prompted personal misgivings to surface. Fact was, no great dream animated my life at the time, and I wondered whether it was sadder not to have a dream at all or to have one that could never be achieved.

When I weighed Red, he registered 123 pounds, down almost fifty pounds from his weight during his previous visit. His blood pressure was higher as well. Red complained that his eyesight was failing and that he hardly had enough energy to go to the bathroom. When I suggested that he get a wheelchair, however, he bristled and told me that it was time to call the undertaker when his feet no longer could take him where he needed to go.

The last part of the exam involved a check of Red's prostate. I couldn't detect any enlargement, and he didn't register any pain. I concluded that whatever was causing Red to wither away would require more diagnostic tools than I had available. As I helped Red put on his shirt, I noticed a spot on the back of his neck, just above his collar, but partially hidden by his straggly gray hair. The spot was the color of a ripe blackberry, and when I rubbed my finger over it, I could tell it was raised slightly above the surrounding skin.

Excusing myself for a minute, I went to Tobias' office to check his skin cancer guide. The irregular dark spot seemed to fit the description of a nodular type of melanoma. Red's previous cancer had been the less serious flat type. Nodular melanoma was far more aggressive and could explain the rapid deterioration in Red's health. I imagined that a lifetime spent outdoors, probably without sunscreen, made Red a likely candidate for recurring skin cancer. Still, I was not a dermatologist. An expert would need to examine Red and probably do a biopsy. If Red's spot turned out to be nodular melanoma and it was causing his weakened condition, I believed it was too late for surgery.

I shared my concerns with Red, but did not mention my pessimism regarding a surgical solution. Then I offered to set up an appointment for him with a specialist in Richmond. Red looked at me as if I had asked him to throw back a prized catch. "Hold on a minute, Doc," he replied while struggling to rise from his chair. "I came here thinking you could help me get my energy back. I wasn't expecting a death sentence."

"Slow down, Red. I just want to have an expert check that spot. If it is malignant, a specialist can remove it before it spreads."

"I had that other spot removed, as you'll recall. The surgeon told me he got it all."

I felt sorry for Red. It was like he brought his truck in for an oil change and discovered it needed a new engine. Only in this case, they no longer made engines for his model. I half-heartedly reassured Red that his spot most likely was not life-threatening, but I knew he didn't buy it. His hands were shaking as he gripped his canes, and he seemed as nervous as a long-tailed cat in a room full of rocking chairs. No matter how many times I dealt with these types of cases, it still upset me to see an old man scared of dying. As a kid, I probably watched too many movies where the aging hero stares down death and laughs in her face. Men like Red are supposed to confront death the way they faced life, with spirit and pugnacity.

"You know, Doc," Red said in a low voice, hardly more than a raspy whisper, "Rachel used to warn me that the day would come when I'd turn to God."

I told Red that he shouldn't jump to premature conclusions, and I reiterated my advice to see a specialist. Red just shook his head and started to leave. Then I said something I probably shouldn't have. I suggested it might be a good idea for him to contact his son and let him know what was going on.

At the mention of Lee, whatever fear had gripped Red evaporated. He flashed an angry look, his back stiffened, and he called out for Rita.

I followed Red to the waiting room, chastising myself for mishandling my patient. As Grace helped Red with his jacket, I pulled Rita aside and filled her in on my concerns. Then I asked if she knew how to contact Red's son. Rita blushed and indicated that she had a phone number in Florida, but added that she hadn't heard from Lee in months. I volunteered to call him myself if she felt uncomfortable doing so, but Rita flashed an enigmatic smile and said she'd been looking for an excuse to contact "the son of a bitch."

Chapter 5

AN ALARMING DISAPPEARANCE

As soon as Red and Rita departed, I phoned the dermatologist that I knew in Richmond. Luckily, she was home on a Saturday. I described the spot on Red's neck, and she confirmed my suspicions, pointing out that nodular melanoma often is found in men who have spent a great deal of time exposed to the sun. Her advice, as I expected, was to get Red to a specialist as soon as possible. She didn't realize, of course, the challenge this advice presented. I sat at my desk for half an hour trying to figure out some way of changing Red's mind. What made my task especially hard was the fact that part of me understood only too well why Red had little interest in seeing a specialist. With the possible exception of his hunting dogs, what reason did he have to continue living?

When I finally left the office it was after five. I considered postponing my visit to the Ashcrofts because I did not want to risk interrupting their dinner. Curiosity, however, trumped good manners, or maybe I just desired gracious company after a difficult afternoon. Whatever the reason, I found myself driving toward Devon as the late afternoon shadows lengthened across the lowlands. The closer I got to Devon, the more I hoped my impromptu visit actually would prompt a dinner invitation. As much as I loved MacDog, my West Highland terrier, he wasn't much for meal-time conversation. The prospect of dining with two delightful people caused me to press the accelerator a little harder than Sheriff "Wild Bill" Rogers would have liked. I was thankful it wasn't later in the evening, when I knew Rogers and his deputies would be lying in wait for speeders and drunk drivers.

No sooner had I pulled into Devon's circular driveway than Gray Emory came running from the mansion in an obvious state of distress. Emory was missing, and she was beside herself with worry. I tried to calm her and asked why she was so sure Emory was missing. She explained that her husband was a creature of routine, and the routine he treasured above all others was what he called "low tea." Come hell or high water, when four-thirty rolled around, Emory expected Gray to join him for a whiskey or two. I recall feeling a slight pang of regret when she added, "It's a very special time for us."

Seeing it was just a few minutes past six, I suggested that Emory probably was out exploring some local cemetery and simply lost track of time. Gray informed me that I obviously did not understand her husband. After an awkward silence, she revealed that Emory had been visibly upset when she shared the news from her California trip.

I asked if that meant Carol Ann and Brad were unwilling to help with Devon's debt problems.

Gray was surprised that I knew why she had gone to California. Emory, I said, shared the purpose of her visit. Gray admitted that she was very disappointed in her daughter. With barely concealed anger, she told me that Carol Ann and Brad had more than enough money to help Emory pay off his loans. Apparently Brad seemed willing to help, but Carol Ann insisted she wanted no part of Devon, at least while her mother resided there. "Be glad you don't have any children," Gray snapped.

It was not the time or the place to inquire further about Carol Ann's reasons for rejecting Gray's plea, so I asked her how she could be so certain Emory had taken her news badly. "Because at first he didn't say anything," she replied. "Silence is a sure-fire indication that my husband is upset." I pressed her to recall everything that happened after she told Emory about Carol Ann's rejection, but I clearly was out of my element. What Gray needed at the moment was a trained detective, not a well-meaning amateur.

After thinking to herself for a minute or two, Gray recalled that Emory said he had some things to reflect on and sort out. "It's certainly not unusual for my husband to make such a comment," she pointed out. "Perhaps you haven't yet discovered that Emory's given to thoughts more than actions, God love him."

I struggled to come up with something constructive to say, but before I could do so, Gray recollected that Emory made a point of thanking her for going to California. "He must have thanked me a dozen times. I guess you've heard how much I hate to fly. And if there's anything I hate worse than flying, it's begging, especially my kin." Gray paused, as if something new had just come to mind. "One more thing, Russell. Emory told me not to worry, that he'd take care of everything." The remark hadn't struck her as odd at the time, but upon reflection, it bothered her.

The remark bothered me as well. When people make up their mind to end it all, they often become surprisingly calm. They focus on others, not themselves. I couldn't help wondering if Emory had decided to end his life so Gray would be free to sell Devon? Naturally I did not share this dark thought with Gray.

Gray asked me if Emory ever mentioned his brother Thomas. I said no. She told me that Emory would be displeased with her for revealing family secrets, but that I needed to know why her fretting was justified. Thomas was two years older than Emory and old Mosby's pride and joy. He had been groomed to take over the day-to-day operation of Devon and restore the Ashcroft fortune. Mosby even admitted to having visions of Thomas one day becoming Governor of the Old Dominion. It was said that before Thomas could chew solid food Mosby had planned his son's life. Thomas would be tutored at home until he was old enough to attend Woodberry Forest. Then he'd go to Charlottesville , earn a degree in commerce, return to Devon, and become active in the Democratic Party. Mosby would make certain Thomas met all the right people, including the "apple pickers" from Winchester.

Gray stopped to light a cigarette, then inhaled deeply. I asked her if we should notify Sheriff Rogers of Emory's absence. Either she didn't hear me or she chose to ignore my question. In any event, Gray concluded her account by saying, "All of Mosby's hopes and dreams for the Ashcroft dynasty were crushed against a bridge abutment on Route 29."

I did not request details, but Gray was intent on giving me the entire story. Mosby had given Thomas a new Buick for his 21st birthday. The young man was a fourth year at the University of Virginia, two years ahead of Emory. Thomas insisted that Emory join him for a run to Sweetbriar College. Thomas always worried that his younger brother spent too much time with his head in a book and not enough time, as Gray put it, with his hand up a skirt. Before leaving Charlottesville, the boys stopped at an ABC store, and Thomas bought a fifth of bourbon. He drank almost half the bottle on the way to Sweetbriar, where he met a girl he had danced with at a mixer and dated several times. She brought along a classmate for Emory, and the two couples drove to Lynchburg for dinner. After dinner the bottle was passed around, and Thomas suggested finding a secluded place to park. The girls nixed the idea because of their curfew, and Thomas reluctantly returned them to their dormitory. Gray told me that Emory never forgave himself for allowing Thomas to drive back to Charlottesville. His brother had drunk much more bourbon than Emory, and he struggled to stay awake. Every time Emory volunteered to take the wheel, Thomas laughed and said he was fine.

When Emory recounted the accident for the State Police, he said Thomas became disoriented by the high beams of an oncoming car and swerved too far to the right. The tires hit loose gravel near an overpass, and Thomas lost control. The Buick crashed into the bridge abutment, and Emory managed to extend his arms to brace himself and absorb some of the impact, but Thomas did not react so quickly. His head struck the steering wheel and snapped back violently. He never regained consciousness.

The death of Mosby's oldest son devastated him, and he blamed Emory for not insisting on driving back to Charlottesville. After the funeral, the old man took Emory aside and told him the only honorable thing to do was to pick up his fallen brother's banner. Mosby, in other words, expected Emory to forget about his dreams of becoming a historian and focus on acquiring the expertise necessary to manage Devon. Emory understood he had no choice in the matter.

A capable diagnostician always trusts his instincts, and mine were beginning to line up with Gray's apprehensions concerning Emory's absence. It was not hard to imagine the pressures building for Emory now that Carol Ann and Brad had refused to offer financial assistance. Emory clearly had experienced more disappointment than a good man deserved. Physicians have no way to gauge how much heartache one person can bear, but I suspected Emory was nearing his limit. I reached out to hold Gray's hand as I stressed what was obvious: there was precious little daylight left. If we were going to search for Emory, we had to begin immediately.

Hurriedly considering how we might proceed, I recalled what Tobias had told me about Mosby's drowning. Releasing Gray's hand, I started running toward the dock. Gray realized what I was thinking and started running as well. We both hoped to find Emory's vintage Chris Craft still tied to its mooring. Instead, what we found was a boatless berth.

The image of Emory's clothed and bloated body bobbing near the shore popped into my head, but I said nothing, instead insisting we call the sheriff and ask his advice about mounting a search. Returning to the house, Gray placed the call while I tracked down Edward. He was in the kitchen putting away glasses, and I asked if he knew where Mr. Emory was. I prayed this was one of those occasions when Edward decided to hear what was being said. Continuing his chores, he calmly told me that Mrs. Gray already had asked the same question. If Edward was worried about what might have happened to his employer, he didn't show it.

Returning to the library, I overheard Gray on the phone arguing with Sheriff Rogers. From what I could tell, Rogers felt it was too soon to form a search party. Gray sternly reminded him of what happened to Emory's father, but apparently he believed it was necessary to wait a bit longer. Gray slammed the receiver down, displaying a tremor of temper I had not previously witnessed nor believed her capable of producing. Suddenly realizing that she was not alone, Gray quickly collected herself and shared her conversation with Sheriff Rogers. Department policy required a twelve-hour wait before organizing a search, except in cases where foul play was evident. "It'll be morning by the time the sheriff does anything," Gray whimpered, barely holding back tears.

It was all I could do not to gather Gray in my arms and comfort her, but such a well-intentioned act, I knew, could easily be misconstrued as taking advantage of a dreadful situation. Instead I suggested we take my Jeep and drive as far as we could along the old farm road that paralleled the James to see if we could spot Emory or his boat. Gray responded that my idea was better than sitting around waiting for the sheriff to act, but then she remembered that the farm road only ran a mile or so in each direction before encountering an unbridged creek. I asked if any of her neighbors had a boat we could borrow. Gray thanked me for trying to be helpful, but reminded me it would be dark by the time we found a boat.

The thought of waiting helplessly for hours was agonizing. Faced with an emergency, I had an almost visceral need to do something, keep busy, anything to avoid waiting helplessly for a possible tragedy to unfold. Clearly, however, there really was nothing constructive that the two of us could accomplish at the moment. We had to wait and, though I'm not a religious man, pray.

Gray asked Edward to bring us some glasses, ice, and bourbon. Normally the Professor would have gone home by this time, but apparently he sensed that Mr. Emory's absence was concerning. Managing a brave smile, Gray asserted that Emory would have approved of raising a glass at such a troubling time. When Edward returned, I offered a toast to Emory's safe return, and Gray gently tapped my glass with hers while avoiding my eyes. As we sipped, we quizzed each other on all the reasons why we should not be worried about Emory. He was, after all, a stable and responsible person. He loved Gray and wouldn't do anything to cause her grief. He knew firsthand what the effects could be when a loved one took his own life. Probably he ran into some neighbors on the River, accepted an invitation for a cocktail, and simply lost track of the time.

Having exhausted our supply of hoped for possibilities, we turned to more personal topics in order to pass the time. Gray asked me why I decided to give up my practice in Richmond and move to Charles City County. I figured Tobias probably had shared my background with her already, but I appreciated the fact that Gray felt comfortable inquiring about my life. I explained how my marriage deteriorated during my residency at MCV. Working eighty-hour weeks left little time for Mary Beth.

When I was home, I either studied my medical texts or slept. Mary Beth filled her time with Junior League and the Garden Club, or so she said. Eventually I discovered she was having an affair with an attending physician she had met at the hospital's annual Christmas party. Seems the son of a bitch always knew when I was tied up at the hospital.

Gray listened as attentively as someone whose husband was missing might be expected to listen. Between glances at the antique clock on the mantle she expressed sympathy for what I had gone through. When I finished, she told me about her first marriage, a "union that never was meant to be" according to her. Her husband was a boy named Billy that she dated in high school. His lofty ambition to become an aeronautical engineer, something unusual among her male classmates, impressed her. Gray and Billy wed a week after graduating from high school, and soon thereafter Carol Ann was born. Hearing this, I surmised that Carol Ann probably had been conceived before wedding bells rang.

The future plans that had drawn Gray to Billy evaporated quickly after Carol Ann was born. He talked about saving enough money to attend college, but Gray realized he was spending what little was left from his weekly paycheck on his car. She blamed herself for making a bad marital decision. "If I knew what I know now," she sighed, "I'd have taken one look at Billy's good-for-nothing old man and put as much distance as I could between us." According to her, Billy's father never earned an honest day's pay in his life. What money he had came from gambling, running cigarettes up north, and convincing elderly folks that they needed unnecessary repairs. In Gray's estimation, Billy was nothing more than "a shadow of a shadow."

As she spoke, I wondered about what Gray was not telling me. People always make choices about what to share and what not to share about themselves. I had failed to tell Gray, for example, that I started an affair with a nurse soon after learning of Mary Beth's indiscretion. My fear was that Gray might think less of me if I added that detail.

So, what important personal information had Gray kept to herself? Emboldened by my second glass of bourbon, I started to ask that very question when the phone rang. Sheriff Rogers called back to ask if Emory had showed up. Apparently he was reconsidering his earlier decision to delay organizing a search.

As Gray repeated what she previously told Rogers, I heard the front door open. Knowing Edward had returned to the kitchen, I rose and went to investigate. With profound relief, I discovered Emory in the entryway removing his jacket. He appeared to be all right, though a little fatigued.

Emory obviously was surprised to see me. His demeanor indicated concern as he asked if anything had happened to Gray. Anxiety gave way to relief when she emerged from the library, hugged him, and explained what had been going on. After scolding her husband for causing such an uproar, she told him about finding his boat missing from the dock and calling Sheriff Rogers. Emory swore he would tell us what happened, but not before pouring himself a stiff drink.

Retiring to the library, Gray and I sat down while Emory emptied the bourbon decanter. Taking a seat next to his wife, he explained that he needed to mull things over when he learned of Carol Ann and Brad's refusal to provide a loan. The best place for serious thought, according to Emory, was on the water. He never intended to miss low tea, but his preoccupation with financial matters caused him to overlook a check of the boat's reserve supply of gasoline. Near Jamestown Island, the Chris Craft sputtered several times and stopped.

Before Emory could finish his story, Gray interrupted and asked if he came up with any answers during his cruise. "Just one," Emory chuckled as he looked me in the eye. "Doc, how'd you like to purchase Devon?" Gray shot back, "Is that the best you could do?" She dabbed her eyes with her handkerchief while Emory sipped his bourbon. Nothing was said for several minutes. Eventually Gray excused herself on the pretense that we all needed a bite to eat along with our drinks. Before leaving the room, she gave me a faint smile and instructed me to come up with a solution to Devon's future by the time she returned.

I couldn't tell if she was kidding, but I was clear on one thing. I had no clue how to bring an ailing plantation back to health. So instead I asked Emory how he'd gotten back up river without gas for his boat. Gray popped her head out of the kitchen to hear her husband's response. After waiting over an hour for a passing boat, Emory said he spotted two fishermen in a small boat with an outboard motor. Turned out they were related in some way to Edward, and they offered him their spare fuel can. It contained just enough gas to get him back home. Emory stood up, pulled some bills from his wallet, and went to the kitchen to ask Edward to repay his relatives for their generosity.

Gray looked at me, and I looked at her, but neither of us spoke. Suddenly she started crying again. I knew that, once a potential crisis passes, people who had maintained their composure sometimes break down. If I hadn't expected Emory to return at any moment, I would have held Gray in my arms and comforted her.

When Emory came back, he looked at both of us and asked what was wrong. Gray explained how worried she had been, though she never mentioned Mosby's probable suicide as the reason for her concern. Emory gave Gray a look of such genuine affection that I almost started crying. How, I wondered, could he muster such compassion with all that he was going through? Taking Gray in his arms, as I wished I could have done, he spoke softly. "I know what you must have been thinking, dear one, but believe me, I've no intention of doing anything foolish."

Emory apologized to me for the awkwardness of the moment and explained that some people felt his father had taken the very same boat from the dock and ended his life. I decided to say nothing about having previously learned of Mosby's drowning from Tobias. Emory stepped back from Gray and held her hand in his. "We still can't be sure Father took his life, my dear. And even if he did, I'm very different from him, as you must know." Emory stressed the word "must."

I was feeling increasingly uncomfortable with the highly personal nature of the conversation, so I excused myself with a fib about needing to return to the office. Emory and Gray escorted me to the door. Before I could step outside, however, Emory put his hand on my shoulder and asked me what I would do if I were him.

I recall thinking, "You should forget about your financial worries for the evening, retire to the bed chamber with your winsome wife, and enjoy each other to the fullest." I didn't express this thought out loud, of course. What I did offer in response to Emory's query was another question. What did he have to lose by investigating the offer that had been made for Devon? I went on to recommend that he insist on meeting with the actual buyer, not his surrogate, so he could clearly convey his concerns regarding Devon's future. No sooner had I shared my thoughts than I had the oddest sensation that Gray disapproved of what I suggested. When she remained in the doorway instead of walking me out to the Jeep with Emory, my feelings were confirmed. I wondered at the time why Gray might be opposed to learning more about the mysterious offer to purchase her home.

Chapter **6**

A VISIT TO RED'S

As the Jeep left Ashcroft property and rumbled back onto Route 5, my mind took a journey of its own, back to other times when my intuition missed the mark. Perhaps I was no more able to guess Gray's desires than I had been able to anticipate Mary Beth's. I recalled one occasion when Mary Beth and I drove home after some Country Club of Virginia function and she seemed disappointed and morose. I surmised that the incessant gossiping and blatantly superficial conviviality had annoyed her. It certainly drained my well. The next day she confided that her upset stemmed from our failure to make what she considered the "right impression" the previous evening. Not being one who ever cared much about what other folks thought, I struggled to understand why impressing a gaggle of strangers mattered so much to my wife.

Speeding along Route 5, my thoughts returned to Gray Ashcroft. Why in the world wouldn't she be overjoyed to sell Devon and be free of its enormous emotional and financial burden? Perhaps I'm just too pragmatic, but her apparent insistence on hanging on to Emory's "ancestral cottage," as he sometimes referred to Devon, made no sense to me.

Typically I make a point of not dwelling on the past or on matters over which I have no control, but I was bothered by both that evening. The more I tried to think about other things, the more I circled back to Mary Beth and Gray. A diversion was called for. Pulling into my driveway, I made up my mind to undertake two therapeutic actions. First, I planned to spend the next day, Sunday, working in my yard. Second, I decided to pay a visit to Red Buchanan after work on Monday and convince him to see a specialist in Richmond.

The next day I rose at the crack of ten, fortified myself with strong coffee, and checked out what needed to be done around my yard. Though I liked domestic chores about as much as rectal exams, I always felt a sense of accomplishment after several hours of puttering and pruning. I chose not to touch my three peach trees, since they just had started to bloom. Emory told me that peach blossoms were a signal to farmers to plant potatoes. As he put it, "The land tells us farmers what to do, if we only look and listen." Sadly, Emory also informed me that he lacked the cash to hire people to plant potatoes. He and Edward planned to tackle the job themselves.

I ended up weeding my driveway and trimming back the rhododendrons that were obscuring the front of my house. After a relaxing bath, I spent the rest of the afternoon reading up on treatments for skin cancer in preparation for the next day's visit to Red's.

After an unremarkable day at the office on Monday, I asked Grace for directions to Red's house. She said he lived off Route 615, beyond Holdcroft, close to where fishermen put in on the Chickahominy River. "Just go east of Blanks Tavern and Binns Hall, then past the old Southall Plantation," she instructed. "You can't miss it."

I've learned the hard way that any time someone says you can't miss something, the odds are nine out of ten you'll miss it. After passing Mount Airy, I realized I was in trouble, so I stopped at the general store in Rustic and called Grace. Fortunately she hadn't left the office. Making no effort to conceal her impatience with me, she said to retrace my steps and look for a dirt road just past the landing at Holdcroft.

When I backtracked, I realized why Red's driveway had eluded me. The rural delivery mailbox had "Buchanan" marked on only the east side, the direction the letter carrier came from. I had driven in from the west. Beneath the mailbox were several newspapers, so I stopped to pick them up for Red. His driveway consisted of two red clay threads running back through the pines. The man apparently valued privacy. After a few hundred yards I came upon a clearing in the middle of which stood a substantial looking two-story brick house with a porch that ran across the front. From the style I guessed it dated from the turn of the nineteenth century, but it looked older. Waist-high grass and weeds surrounded the house, making it look abandoned. I surmised Red had been doing poorly for some time.

When my knocks went unanswered, I wondered whether Red had gone somewhere with Rita. Or worse. Would I be the one who discovered his body? I stood on the porch debating whether to enter the house when I heard a faint voice say, "That you, Rita?" I identified myself, and a few moments later the voice told me to enter. I was greeted by two large hunting dogs intent on sniffing me to make sure I meant no harm. "You needn't fear Biscuit and Gravy, Doc," Red called out, though I still couldn't see where Red was in the living room. No light was on, and the curtains were drawn shut. My eyes finally adjusted, and I saw Red sitting in a recliner, half hidden under a brown quilt that blended with the chair. Biscuit and Gravy dutifully returned to their posts on each side of Red's recliner. Red apologized for the place being such a mess and said he hoped Rita would excuse his lousy housekeeping. Forcing a smile, he asked if I dropped by because I needed a fishing guide.

I laughed and told him I wasn't much for fishing, but if I ever got a hankering to drop a line, he'd be the first person I'd contact. Red advised me not to wait too long, and I replied that my visit was intended to ensure he'd enjoy a lot more days of fishing.

I pulled up a chair and sat next to Red. He knew, of course, why I'd dropped by. "You're going to try and talk me into going to Richmond to get that spot checked, aren't you?" I nodded and repeated what I told him in the office about the spot possibly being linked to how poorly he was feeling. Seeing Red's weakened condition made me almost certain the spot was cancerous; however, if that were the case and the cancer was melanoma, seeing a specialist most likely would be a waste of time. Still, I'd been wrong enough times to realize the value of a second opinion. There was at least a chance the spot was a mole of some kind and Red simply had contracted a viral infection.

Red tried to change the subject by pointing out that I was sitting in Rachel's favorite chair. She could knit up a storm in that chair, he observed, especially if the Grand Ole Opry was on the radio. Red continued to share stories about how wise and wonderful Rachel had been. Clearly the man was lost without her. The more stories he told, the more I understood why he was so uninterested in prolonging his life. Here was a man racked with pain, but totally at peace with the knowledge that soon he would be reunited with his beloved wife.

When Red tired of talking, the two of us just sat in the gloomy silence of the living room. Biscuit and Gravy never left their master's side. After several minutes passed, I looked Red straight in his half-closed eyes and asked, "Is there nothing I can say to convince you to see a specialist?"

Red just shook his head, then mustered enough strength to tell me that he appreciated my concern, but that he was prepared for nature to take its course. "Dust to dust, like they say, Doc." Red started coughing and spat several times into his handkerchief. Even in the dim light, I could tell he was coughing up blood.

We sat in silence a bit longer. I brought Red some water to drink. After taking a sip, Red delivered his benediction. "I've pretty much lived the life I wanted, Doc. That might surprise a highly educated man like yourself, but it's true. Lee never would believe me when I told him I didn't want nothing I didn't already have."

I told Red that I envied him and understood why my pleas were unlikely to change his mind. I wasn't so sure that, under similar circumstances, I wouldn't have made the same decision.

"Look here," Red gestured around him. "I'm living in the house my granddaddy built with his own two hands. He was a crackerjack mason if there ever was one. Taught me everything I know. Not just about laying bricks neither. Daddy taught me about hunting and fishing, just about all a man needed to know to survive off the land. And then there's Rachel. Couldn't have asked for a better companion. Salt of the earth. And a dash of pepper, too!"

Red went on to say he read the newspaper and watched television, so he realized what was going on in cities and around the world. That's why he understood how truly fortunate he had been. Then he added softly, "My only regret is not doing a better job with Lee."

Since my efforts to help Red medically weren't going anywhere, I decided to shift my visit to a purely social one. Strange though it may sound, I found comfort in Red's words, even though they cast my own life in a questionable light. Wanting to learn more about him, I asked, "What happened with Lee?"

Red took a few sips of water and explained that no father could have been any more proud of a son than he had been of Lee. Lee excelled in high school, lettering in three sports and graduating near the top of his class. William and Mary offered him a scholarship to play baseball, and he accepted, but he never got the hang of college life. Red suspected his boy felt like a fish out of water around the rich kids from Richmond and Northern Virginia. Rachel had been of the opinion that Lee missed Rita, his high school sweetheart, more than he cared to admit.

Whatever the reason, Lee up and quit William and Mary at the end of his freshman year and returned home to look for a job. Rita was upset that Lee had squandered an opportunity to make something of himself. She blamed herself for Lee's decision and fretted that he might be drafted and sent to Vietnam. Lee and Rita fought all the time. Finally she had enough and broke off their relationship, telling Lee that she had no intention of being the reason he never amounted to anything. Lee took it very hard. When Rita moved away to find a job, Lee enlisted in the Army. Rachel swore he did it to spite Rita.

No sooner had Lee finished basic training than he shipped out to Vietnam. Rachel was never the same, according to Red. She worried the entire time Lee was overseas. Couldn't hold down food and rarely got a good night's rest. As it turned out, Lee came back with a dozen decorations and nary a scratch. He became a local hero. By that time, Rita had returned, and she and Lee became "real serious," as Red put it. Too serious, I guess, because Rita got pregnant.

At this point in the story, Red's tone changed. The pride so evident in his earlier remarks was displaced by disappointment and, I detected, a dash of anger. Lee was not ready to be a father and pressed Rita to get an abortion. He came to Red and asked to borrow money for the procedure. Red and Rachel had a long talk about the matter. Rachel was adamant that Rita should have the baby and that Lee should marry her. The whole affair took a toll on everyone. Lee blamed Red for not supporting him and stormed off, vowing to have nothing more to do with his father. When Rita considered having the baby and giving it up for adoption, Lee told her he needed to get out of Charles City County for good. Everybody knows each other's business in a place like this, and Lee just couldn't handle the embarrassment of getting Rita pregnant and then not keeping the child.

No sooner did Lee leave than Rita up and went to her sister's in West Virginia. She never disclosed to anyone what she actually did about the pregnancy. All Red knew was that by the time Rita returned nearly a year later, Rachel had gotten very sick. She complained of being abandoned by the God to whom she prayed nightly for a grandchild. The ensuing months spent watching Rachel wither away were the hardest of Red's life.

My conversations with Red and Gray Ashcroft caused me to be thankful I didn't have any children and also to wonder whether my parents had experienced such heartache with me. I thought of Gray's daughter and how she wanted to have as little to do as possible with her mother. What was it with these children? They're grown-ups after all. Couldn't they see past their own selfish interests and realize how much they owed their parents? What chance do we have of creating a compassionate, caring world if children can't get along with their parents?

Red sensed that I was mulling over something and asked what was on my mind, but I saw that he was exhausted. I got up to leave, but hesitated as I opened the door and asked Red if he wanted me to track down Lee and tell him his father was ill. Suddenly Red sat up and snapped, "Just let me go in peace, Doc."

My drive home that evening found me paying much more attention to my visit with Red than to the road. I narrowly missed an old man walking along the road as well as two young deer. It troubled me to think of reaching a point where I, like Red, preferred to exit more than to exist. Would Red have been willing to seek medical help, I wondered, if Lee were still part of his life? I had to believe the answer would have been yes.

When I arrived home, I fed MacDog, let him out to pee, and checked my answering service. I wanted to phone Rita, but it was pretty late. Nonetheless, I needed to know if she had been able to reach Lee in Florida. Rita answered the phone, saying, "Lee, is that you?" She apologized when I identified myself, and I followed with an apology for calling so late.

Making no effort to conceal her anger, Rita told me she phoned a Florida number that Lee had given one of his old high school buddies in case the guy, a local mechanic, wanted to join him in the Sunshine State. A woman answered the phone, which didn't sit too well with Rita. According to this woman, Lee had signed on to be a crew member with an outfit sailing from Key West to Barbados. He wasn't due back for several days, and she had no idea how to reach him. Rita told the woman that Lee's father was very sick and that he should come home as soon as possible. The woman sounded surprised, saying that Lee claimed both his parents were dead.

I informed Rita of the visit with Red and my concern about his unwillingness to seek medical help. "Those Buchanans are as headstrong as a Baptist missionary," was Rita's exasperated reply. Our frustrations over Red and Lee eventually gave way to speculation. I guessed that Red had very little time left, perhaps a week, a month at most. My prediction was based primarily on Red's physical appearance, the persistent cough, and his lack of desire to go on living. Rita asked me what we should do. Morphine, I suggested, could be prescribed to ease Red's pain, but only if she was willing to administer the medication. Otherwise there wasn't much to be done. I also recommended that Rita get Red to sign a "Power of Attorney" form granting her the authority to make decisions for him when he no longer was capable of doing so.

Before hanging up, Rita asked, "Doc, have you ever longed for something that was hopeless?" Only now can I admit that the first thing that came to mind was Gray Ashcroft. At the time, however, I told Rita only that I had harbored such feelings, but that an ample glass of bourbon worked well as an antidote.

Chapter 7

THE OFFER

The morning after my visit to Red's, I asked Tobias if he'd cover for me over the coming weekend. I had not taken a break since early January, and that escape only resulted in unanticipated tension. A nurse from Williamsburg that I occasionally dated had accepted my invitation to fly to the Bahamas for a long weekend. From botched plane reservations to lousy hotel accommodations to crowded restaurants and finally to awkwardness about sleeping together, the entire junket produced frustration and regret instead of relaxation and intimacy.

Determined to avoid such disappointments, I decided to travel alone by car to the Eastern Shore of Virginia and stay in a waterfront cottage owned by one of my patients. The price was right – free, the company manageable – myself, and the setting uncomplicated and uncrowded – beach and bay. There was something about the austerity of the Eastern Shore that promised much needed serenity. I have always been drawn to remote and impoverished settings where people lust and laugh in spite of their troubles and the environment has not been overly defiled by the hand of man.

I was feeling upbeat about my impending journey when Grace told me that Emory Ashcroft was on the phone. I gently scolded her for not forwarding the call to Tobias, but she covered the receiver and whispered that Mr. Emory was not calling about a medical problem. My first thought was that something had happened to Gray, but when I spoke to Emory, he asked if he could take me up on my offer. I struggled to recall what offer I had made, but for the life of me I couldn't think of anything. Emory sensed my bewilderment because he quickly added, "Let me clarify. I'm referring to the offer I knew you'd make if you realized my circumstances."

Instead of getting upset, I just laughed. Clearly something serious was on Emory's mind, but he didn't allow his worries to subvert his sense of humor. I decided to play along, telling him that I did not own a set of dueling pistols, but if he needed a second, I'd be glad to assist. Without a moment's hesitation, he responded, "I always said that if I had to face death, I wanted a physician at my side…or preferably in front of me."

We carried on this banter a bit longer and then Emory returned to his request. Seems he had taken my advice and called the lawyer who contacted him regarding an offer to purchase Devon. Emory explained to the man that he would never consider selling his ancestral home without meeting the actual buyer. The lawyer agreed to pass along this information to his client. Apparently a few minutes earlier, the lawyer had phoned Emory to say his client could meet on Saturday.

I immediately sensed what was coming and what was going. My trip to the Eastern Shore would have to be postponed if I agreed to hold Emory's hand. He acknowledged the imposition on our fledgling friendship, but I knew he would never ask such a favor unless he really needed my support. Under the circumstances, I could not refuse his request. I was relieved to learn, however, that the meeting with the prospective buyer was planned for 11:30 on Saturday morning at Devon. If it didn't run too long, I'd still be able to reach Onancock by mid-afternoon. Furthermore, I could wait to return until Monday morning. That way, I'd still enjoy two nights away.

As Emory was thanking me, I reminded him that I was a physician, not a financial advisor. He laughed and told me it was moral support he required, not financial advice. Then he suggested that I arrive a little before 11:30.

Saturday dawned one of those glorious spring mornings in

Virginia when the smell of new vegetation blended perfectly with the aroma of coffee. A light southerly breeze promised warmth. Just the kind of morning to force a man to his knees to thank God he lives in the Old Dominion. As I sipped my coffee and read the depressing news from Vietnam in the Richmond Times-Dispatch, I thought about what a stark contrast it would be if I awoke in Saigon that morning.

My friends credit me with having a vivid imagination, but I know my talents fall short when it comes to imagining what it must feel like to fear for your life every moment of the day and night, to never know when the next person you meet might question your loyalties and shoot you in the temple at close range. I put the newspaper aside, unwilling to sully this magnificent morning any further with dark thoughts. Instead I wandered out the back door and admired my yard.

My place is no riverfront plantation, but it has character and some would even say charm, like a Cotswold crofter's home. The previous owners, an elderly Australian couple who moved to the Virginia Piedmont to be closer to their son and his family, took meticulous care of the property, creating meandering gravel paths leading to a sundial, a wildflower patch, and a teak replica of a Jefferson bench. Sitting on the bench to finish my third cup of coffee, I reflected on what Emory might be thinking at that moment. Selling one's ancestral home had to be painful, but perhaps it might also be liberating.

Later that morning, I honored Emory's request and arrived at Devon a few minutes before 11:30. As I drove past the stables, Gray's Lincoln roared past me in the opposite direction. I waved, but the glare of the sun prevented me from seeing whether she returned my greeting. I slowed, thinking she might stop and back up, but all I saw in the rearview mirror was a cloud of dust. After parking in front of the mansion, I noticed Emory walking slowly toward the River. Hearing my door slam, he turned around and headed back.

"Russell, you're a man of your word."

"I'm glad to help in any way I can," I responded. "Where was Gray going? She flew by me. Doesn't she want to meet the mysterious buyer?"

Emory hesitated for a moment. "I'm afraid she had another

commitment. She asked me to thank you for coming. We're both terribly grateful."

The two of us chatted casually for a few minutes about all the things that needed fixing around Devon. For a moment, in fact, it almost seemed as if Emory was trying to convince himself that he'd be better off without the place. When I inquired about his strategy for the morning's meeting, he assured me he had no plans to do anything but meet the buyer and hear his proposal. As he explained what he told the buyer's lawyer over the phone, we heard the sound of an approaching vehicle. A black Mercedes pulled up, parked, and both front doors opened simultaneously. A short, overweight white man, probably in his late fifties, climbed out of the passenger's side, and a tall, trim black man wearing sunglasses got out of the driver's side.

Emory and I jumped to the same conclusion, but he was first to verbalize it. "Did our mysterious buyer decide to remain mysterious?" Emory asked the overweight white man.

"Not at all," answered the black man with a hint of annoyance. "Allow me to introduce myself. My name is Henry Brown." He extended his hand toward Emory.

Emory mechanically shook his hand, though I suspect he, like myself, was too stunned to register what he was doing.

"Your reaction explains why I preferred to remain anonymous," Brown chuckled. "Let me introduce my attorney, Arthur Allen."

Emory shook Allen's hand and introduced me. The four of us then walked into the mansion. As we did, I overheard Brown whisper to his attorney, "I never thought I'd be entering Devon through the front door." I knew Emory also heard the remark, but he chose not to comment.

We gathered in the library, and Emory asked Edward to bring us coffee. I couldn't help wondering what Edward must have thought about serving someone of his own race in Devon's library. If this presumably unique experience prompted a reaction from Edward, however, it never registered on his face. He remained impassive as always, apparently unimpressed by the guests and uninterested in their reason for visiting.

Skipping pleasantries, Allen addressed Emory as soon as Edward departed. "Let me get right to the point, Mr. Ashcroft."

It occurred to me that Allen must be from up north. No son of Virginia ever got "right to the point" upon first meeting a stranger.

"We know," Allen continued, "that your farm has been struggling for some time. My client, Mr. Brown, is prepared to make what I regard as a very attractive offer for the property."

"Hold on, Mr. Allen," Emory interjected. "It doesn't really matter what you consider to be an attractive offer, does it? I don't know you, and I don't know your client." I started to wonder whether the only reason Emory consented to this meeting was a purely academic interest in what kind of person would consider purchasing Devon and for what reason. Was he simply playing out his love of history, adding another page to the chronicle of Devon that he hoped one day to write?

Emory asked Brown why he was so interested in purchasing Devon. He looked only at Brown, as if Allen had forfeited his role as intermediary by being too blunt.

"They tell me, Mr. Ashcroft," Brown began, "you're something of a historian in these parts. Have you run across one of my ancestors, a man named Solomon Profitt?"

Emory shook his head and replied that the name was unfamiliar.

"That surprises me because your great grandfather owned my great grandfather."

To say I felt uneasy at this point is to risk understatement. I suddenly regretted my suggestion that Emory meet Mr. Brown.

To Emory's credit, he took no visible offense at Brown's remark. Ever the lover of local history, Emory instead appropriated the revelation as an opportunity to learn more about Brown's lineage. We found out that Brown's great grandfather and great grandmother had been young children at Devon before the Civil War. When McClellan occupied the plantation during the Peninsula Campaign, some of Devon's enslaved people took off for Fort Monroe and what they hoped would be free passage north. Brown's ancestors, however, decided not to escape. After the war, Solomon Profitt worked out a sharecropping agreement with Emory's great grandfather. Brown's great grandmother went to work near Williamsburg as a domestic servant, but she eventually returned to Devon to marry Profitt. The couple had three children, one that died in infancy, a daughter named Callie Profitt, and John Mercer Profitt, Henry's grandfather.

John Profitt realized there was no future in sharecropping and talked his father into letting him attend the newly opened St. Emma's Industrial and Agricultural School in Powhatan County. When he completed his course of study, John sought his fortune in Richmond rather than return to Charles City County, where the opportunities for blacks were limited mostly to farm work. He settled in Fulton, a working class settlement along the north side of the James River. Fulton was a common point of entry for rural blacks moving to Richmond. It had the advantage of being located near the railroad yards where a large number of blacks found jobs offering better wages than those available to farm hands.

John Profitt's dream was to make enough money to purchase land in Charles City County. He swore, in fact, that he would not return to his native county until he could be a landowner. It was an oath he never fulfilled. Despite his training at St. Emma's, John only found menial work on the railroad. He eventually advanced to gandy dancer, which required him to travel up and down a section of line with a repair crew. When they spotted rotting ties and damaged rails, they replaced them.

In 1908 John met and married a Richmond woman, Ester Brooks, and the couple had three children: Mary Mercer, Jefferson Jasper, and Sarah Solomon Profitt. Mary Mercer married Joseph Brown, a well-to-do undertaker in Jackson Ward. Jackson Ward was a major step up the social ladder from Fulton and a bustling community with many black-owned businesses and a register of important residents. Mary and Joseph had a son, Henry Mercer Brown, and a daughter, Sarah Josephine Brown. The two children attended Armstrong High School, the pride of Richmond's black community. At her debutantes ball, Sarah met her future husband, a Baltimore banker, and the two settled in Maryland. Henry, meanwhile, attended Virginia State University, graduating with honors in 1957. He then went to law school at Howard University, completing his studies in 1960 and returning to Richmond to practice.

At various points in Brown's narrative, Emory interrupted to ask for additional information. What had been Solomon Profitt's responsibilities at Devon? Did he know how to write and, if so, did he leave behind any letters? What land at Devon did he sharecrop? Was John Mercer Profitt named after John Mercer Langston, the remarkable son of a slave owner and a former slave who became a lawyer, a college president, an ambassador, and a Virginia Congressman?

At first Brown seemed to appreciate Emory's interest in his ancestors, but I sensed after a while that he was growing impatient with the barrage of questions. Brown concluded his family history by noting that he and his wife recently had their first child, John Henry Brown. For years they believed they could have no children of their own. When John Henry was born, Brown decided the time had come to fulfill his grandfather's dream of owning property in Charles City County.

"I want my son," Brown declared, "to know that a descendant of slaves can own the very plantation where his ancestors were chattel."

At this point there was an awkward lull in the conversation. The next person to speak was Allen. "Are you willing, Mr. Ashcroft, to give my client's offer serious consideration? I can assure you that there will be no problem with the financial arrangements on our end. I also have studied the figures for farm sales in the area, and I am of the opinion that the amount Mr. Brown is willing to pay is more than fair."

Emory looked fleetingly at Allen before fixing his gaze on Brown. "Land can certainly be valued, Mr. Brown, but legacy is priceless."

"All well and good, but legacy doesn't put food on the table or gasoline in the tank, Mr. Ashcroft. We know about your difficulties."

Although he made no inquiry at the time, Emory confronted me later and expressed surprise that Brown knew about his financial circumstances. I had the distinct impression that he believed I had somehow tipped him off.

Emory declined to confirm Brown's comment about his finances and instead asked him what he was prepared to do to put

Devon back on its feet. Brown smiled and asked why he should share such information when Emory could simply appropriate it for his own benefit. Emory complimented Brown for being a shrewd businessman, then stated that he himself was too committed a fisherman to abandon casting after losing a lure. We all laughed. Emory then speculated that Brown might be thinking of selling off parcels of Devon's property to developers.

Brown studied Emory for several moments before saying, "If that's what concerns you, Mr. Ashcroft, rest assured I have no intention of converting my people's land into a sub-division or retirement community for rich white folks."

Emory bristled at the reference to Devon as the land of Brown's ancestors. I sensed the time had come for me to step in, so I inquired as to whether Brown and his family intended to live at Devon if they purchased the plantation. Brown immediately became defensive and shot back, "Does that bother you, Dr. Curry? Is Charles City County not ready for a black family on the River?"

I was offended by Brown's insinuation, but resisted the temptation to say something rude. Instead, I observed that Emory's concern involved the possibility that Devon might fall into the hands of people with no respect for its history. I fully expected Brown to claim that Devon's history was unworthy of respect, but he simply nodded in agreement, rose from his chair, and informed me that he did not intend to dishonor Devon or its heritage. Then he added, "Have no fear, Dr. Curry. I have the deepest respect for the history of this plantation and the hundreds of human beings who made it possible for the Ashcrofts to become and remain influential and wealthy." I glanced at Emory and caught him wincing at the remark. Brown turned to Allen and suggested they leave and give Mr. Ashcroft time to consider his offer.

As he ushered the two visitors into the wide corridor running the width of the mansion, Emory instantly shifted persona from a defensive property owner to a gracious host. He thanked his guests for taking time from their busy schedules to drive over from Richmond. On the way to the front door, he pointed to portraits of his ancestors and an indentation in the woodwork made by a stray musket ball. Then suddenly he reverted to defensive property owner.

"You know, Mr. Brown, this place has never been listed with any realtor. Perhaps before I do anything rash, I should test the real estate market."

Brown immediately looked at Allen, and Allen looked back at Brown, as if to get instructions about what to say. I thought to myself that Emory was one wily old son-of-a-bitch.

Brown whispered something to Allen, who then said to Emory, "That would be, in my judgment, a big mistake, Mr. Ashcroft."

Emory responded that Allen might be right, but he still felt the need to explore all possible options before making a decision of such magnitude. Allen then asked when Emory might give Brown an answer regarding his offer. Emory ignored the query, but replied that he needed at least a week or two to make up his mind about involving a realtor.

As Brown and Allen departed, Emory put his hand on my shoulder and requested that I walk with him toward the riverbank. I dreaded the prospect of being asked what he should do with Brown's offer. Emory, however, did not solicit my opinion, but instead admitted being embarrassed by assuming that Allen was the buyer and Brown was his chauffeur. I agreed that the faux pas was unfortunate. Then Emory added, "My father would never have committed such an indiscretion."

"From what I've heard of your father," I replied, "he never would have allowed a black man to enter Devon by the front door."

Emory offered a wry smile, then asked me what I would do about Brown's offer if I were in his shoes. I did not want to share what I was thinking. Living with my ex-wife had taught me the dangers of helping someone else make up their mind. If things didn't work out as expected, I'd be the one to bear the blame. I recalled with bitterness when Mary Beth asked my advice about whom to invite to her annual New Year's Eve bash at the Commonwealth Club.

I suggested inviting some single individuals as well as the usual couples. Singles, I reasoned, make a party more lively. She took my advice. It turned out that one of the single women Mary Beth invited was having an affair with the husband of one of the couples. When his wife saw the woman, she created a big scene that was later reported in the local paper's gossip column. According to Mary Beth, I ruined her party and embarrassed her as the hostess.

Feeling that a non-answer was preferable to a wrong answer, I responded to Emory's request by suggesting that he consult with Gray about what to do. He just shoved his hands into his coat pockets and walked back to the mansion without saying a word.

Chapter 8

A QUIET HOMEGOING

The trip to the Eastern Shore offered a brief but much-needed respite from the pressures of my practice. I only can endure so many doses of other people's pain and suffering before I feel compelled to prescribe some solitude for myself. In truth, though, it wasn't just the medical demands that left me spent. I was emotionally exhausted from worrying about Gray and Emory.

My getaway goals were simple. Indulge myself with a trashy novel, take a hike or two, and shoot some photographs. I prefer black and white photography, and the Eastern Shore presents an assortment of unique challenges. For one, there is invariably a lot of interesting background – endless skies, wonderful water vistas – and very little of interest in the foreground. When I hung several of my favorite photographs in the office, Grace informed me that I needed more color in my photographs as well as my life. Picasso had his blue period. I suppose I'm in my black and white period.

My appreciation for the restorative powers of the Eastern Shore began during the dying days of my marriage. The simplicity of the place, with its shoreline, marshes, and pine barrens uninterrupted by any corrupting traces of civilization, was the ideal antidote for the complex world I had to negotiate back home in

Richmond.

No sooner did I start driving east along the Interstate toward Hampton Roads and the Chesapeake Bay Bridge-Tunnel than I found myself once again thinking about Gray and Emory. Emory's strange behavior before I left Devon the previous day bothered me, as did Gray's absence from the meeting with Henry Brown and his lawyer. The more I dwelled on these matters, the madder I got at myself for spoiling my brief break. The medical training I received regarding how to maintain emotional detachment seemed to have been wasted, at least when it came to the Ashcrofts. I kept asking myself why I should care so much about their circumstances, and I kept failing to come up with an answer, at least an answer I'd admit to.

By the time I reached Norfolk, I was fretting about Red Buchanan as well as the Ashcrofts. Having no children of my own, I couldn't claim to be an expert on the dynamics between a father and a son. I had been a son, of course, and despite my share of disagreements with my father, I knew that I wanted to be at his side during his final days. Rita hopefully would be able to reach Lee in time for him to hasten home and work through any unresolved issues with his father.

By the time I reached the mid-point of the Bay Bridge-Tunnel, I recall having an epiphany of sorts. There I was in the middle of the Chesapeake Bay, unable to see the land from whence I came and the land to which I was headed. I was exhilarated by an overwhelming sense of detachment, adrift from my work, my past, and the Ashcrofts. This liberating sensation of total freedom unfortunately lasted no more than a few moments. As the lowlands of Cape Charles came into view, thoughts of worldly matters once again intruded. They remained with me, unwelcome traveling companions, for the duration of my brief escape. Not even an artery-clogging dinner of deep-fried fish and shrimp at a local seafood shack could dispel my concerns.

Early Monday morning I arose and headed back to the reality I never really managed to leave behind. Grace handed me a message as soon as I walked into the office, then proceeded to inform me of its contents before I could read it. Rita had been trying to reach me since 7:00 a.m. Red was not doing very well. Tobias agreed to handle my two scheduled appointments and any walk-ins so that I could make a house call at Red's.

While driving over to Red's, I thought about his stubborn insistence on not going to see a specialist. He must have sensed that his condition was irreversible. Why spend your last days commuting back and forth to a medical center, listening to grave assessments and instructions to make the necessary arrangements? I truly believe that many individuals know when their time has come and harbor no desire to prolong the inevitable. What frightens them is not the prospect of drawing their final breath, but the unknown pain that might accompany it. I brought enough morphine in my medical bag to see that Red slipped away peacefully.

Rita rushed out to greet me as I pulled into Red's driveway. She thanked me for coming so quickly and told me that Red was unable to eat and struggled to catch his breath. Then she added that Lee had phoned from Florida. Red was informed of the call, but she was unsure he understood her, since he seemed to drift in and out of consciousness. Rita told me that Lee was driving up from Florida and planned to arrive sometime the next day. She grabbed my hand as she pleaded for me to keep Red alive until Lee got there. I promised to do what I could and indicated that I brought morphine to ease his pain.

When we reached the front door, Rita paused. "You know," she whispered, "I just don't understand Lee and me. When we're apart, we seem to genuinely care for each other, but put us back together for more than a few days and we start nitpicking and griping. If we know anything in this silly old world, it's how to get on each other's nerves."

I remember desperately wanting to offer Rita some kind of useful nostrum, but being unable to think of anything helpful. All that came to mind was the realization that, where relationships were concerned, I was in need of serious therapy.

Crossing the threshold and staring into the dimly lit room, I immediately knew that Rita had correctly assessed Red's condition. The poor man was hardly visible beneath the quilt on the bed that had been moved into the living room. In the few days since I last saw him, Red had lost color and weight. The pallid flesh on his face hung loosely to his skull like an ill-fitted Halloween mask. Red's ever-loyal hunting dogs, Biscuit and Gravy, stretched out, one on each side of the bed, like a pair of miniature sphinxes guarding the entrance to some backwoods tomb.

Rita sat down beside the bed and gently stroked Red's forehead. Then she got another pillow and placed it under his head to prop it up while she explained that I brought some medicine to ease his pain. Red slowly turned toward me and stared for a moment before recognizing me. Even the slightest movement on his part seemed labored.

I told Red that Rita requested that I drop by. Next, I checked his pulse and blood pressure, which confirmed my initial impression. When I asked him to describe his pain on a scale from one to ten, he just shook his head but said nothing. Eventually, in a raspy voice that was barely audible, Red informed me that he was "right with the Lord and ready to join Rachel." After catching his breath, he added, "If you can speed things along, Doc, I'd be much obliged." Red's arm reached out from beneath the quilt and rested weightless on my hand. "Easing my pain's okay, I guess, but don't prolong my dying. It's homegoing time."

I took a small bottle of morphine from my bag, asked Red to open his mouth, and deposited a few drops under his tongue.

Red told me Rachel made the quilt that covered him when she was pregnant with Lee and that he'd slept under it ever since she passed away. He then looked off to some place neither Rita nor I could see. Rita clutched Red's hand and told him again that Lee was coming soon, but he did not acknowledge her remark.

I motioned for Rita to accompany me into the kitchen and told her that Red had very little time left. The morphine, I explained, would cause him to be in a semi-sedated state until it wore off. If he seemed to be in distress, we could administer more morphine. At some point, probably within a day or two, he would simply stop breathing.

Tears welled up in Rita's eyes, and she looked at me in an odd way. "Doc, I'm sure Red heard me say that Lee was coming. And you know what? I'll bet you a bottle of Wild Turkey that Red is doing everything in his power to die before Lee gets here."

"Why on Earth would he do such a thing," I responded.

"Because I think Red wants to teach the son of a bitch a lesson. Aren't fathers always trying to teach their sons something?"

"I wouldn't know, Rita.

Rita's face flushed with embarrassment. She asked if I'd like a cup of tea, and I nodded. When the tea was ready, we took our cups to Red's bedside and commenced the death watch. I wasn't sure if I did or didn't want Red to hang on long enough to say goodbye to his son. What if seeing Lee really upset Red? I hated the thought that a decent man's last moments might be filled with acrimony.

At least I was certain of one thing. The more I got to know Rita, the more I realized what a rare individual she was. Her compassion was genuine, not phony like all those friends of my ex-wife who bragged about how much they donated to charity. Nary a one of them would have given up a golf game or shopping trip to sit by a dying man's bedside and comfort him. Rita possessed another quality I had come to value above all others – loyalty. As far as I knew, her loyalty did not result from neediness. She was an independent person with the guts to prefer being alone to settling for some pathetic on-again, off-again excuse for a relationship.

Rita caught me off guard when she asked what I was thinking. I almost admitted that my thoughts were about her, but I caught myself. Still, I suspect she might have known because she blushed when I hesitated to respond.

For the next few hours we sat mostly in silence, occasionally breaking the spell that envelops the act of dying to note some slight change in Red's demeanor. At one point, Rita went into the kitchen to put food in the dogs' bowls, but when she called the dogs to come eat, both remained at Red's bedside. Several times Rita shared a fond memory of Red and Rachel. Tea eventually gave way to bourbon, a switch we both agreed would have been endorsed by our quiet companion. Every half hour or so I checked Red's pulse. Once when he appeared to be in pain, I administered more morphine. During this entire time Red never uttered a word. Rita's frequent checking of the clock on the mantle told me she was worried about Lee's race with the grim reaper. Just after sunset Red finally struggled to say something, but neither Rita nor I could make out what it was. His breathing was becoming harder to detect.

Seeing that Rita's spirits were flagging, I tried to strike up a conversation. "What do you think Red might say to Lee if he makes it home in time?"

Rita replied in the most aching voice I ever heard. "He's just got to get here in time, Doc. For his own sake as well as Red's." She slowly shook her head as if she were expressing her disapproval to a young child. "He did so much for that boy that Lee never even realized."

For all the good I was doing, I probably should have gone home, but an inner voice insisted that I stay. Maybe it was some dark desire to witness the father and son reunion. Or perhaps it was simply the comfort I felt in Rita's company. How different Rita was from Gray Ashcroft. When I was around Gray, I felt aroused and jealous of Emory. With Rita, I felt serene. I distinctly recall hoping that someone like Rita would be at my own bedside when the time came.

Rita suggested we change the sheets on Red's bed. I lifted the body, as light as a child's, while being careful to leave Red's beloved quilt covering him. There was so little substance to Red, in fact, that I had the eerie sensation some portion of his being already had departed. Rita changed the sheets, and I placed Red back on the bed. Around ten o'clock, I decided to take the dogs for a short walk. They had hardly budged since late morning. Neither one had eaten anything or gone out to pee. The only time they whimpered was when Red shifted in bed or moaned in pain. I knew that they did not want to leave their master's bedside, but they yielded to me when Rita urged them to go outside and do their business. The fog off the River had come up and was so thick I worried the dogs might wander off. If they did, I'd never be able to find them, but to my relief they accomplished what they needed to do and quickly returned to the front porch.

As the three of us entered the living room, I saw Rita leaning over Red with his hand in hers. My first thought was that he had died, but then I noticed that Rita's head was bent to the side in an effort to hear what Red was struggling to say. Biscuit and Gravy resumed their positions on each side of the bed, while I remained at the door, not wanting to interrupt. I admit trying to overhear what Red was saying, but all I made out were the words "grave" and "clean." Rita picked up a wet washcloth and placed it gently on Red's forehead. As she did, she whispered, "Don't leave now, Red. Hold on just a little longer. For Lee's sake." She started softly crying. "Lee's coming, Red."

Red did not respond.

All of a sudden both dogs commenced a mournful baying sound. Rita stroked Red's hand and kept repeating, "Lee's coming. Lee's coming."

The dogs stood on their hind legs and placed their front paws on the bed, trying to lick Red's face one last time. Eventually they settled down and resumed their guardian posts. I noted the time of death at 11:11 p.m. Rita and I looked at each other, then I walked over and hugged her. "He was like a father to me, " she sobbed. "I've never known a gentler soul."

"I wish I had known him better," I added.

Rita and I had another glass of bourbon, this time toasting Red and Rachel's reunion. Rita started crying again when she thought about how disappointed Lee would be when he arrived. I thought about my own inadequacy at a time like this. It is the physician's curse that death, which is such a unique experience for each individual, comes to be regarded in the aggregate as predictable and commonplace, as integral a part of life's journey as discontent and forgetfulness.

After a while, Rita quieted and I gathered up my things and told her I'd contact the undertaker. She reminded me that Red wanted to be cremated and have his ashes scattered on the River. I assured her that I would make Red's wishes known. As I was leaving Rita took hold of my hand and said how much my presence meant to her.

I looked at Rita, her eyes red from crying and her face drawn from fatigue, and felt a longing that was completely inappropriate under the circumstances. Then I recalled wanting to ask her something. "What was Red saying to you when I returned with the dogs?"

She told me that Red had made a strange request, to please make sure a certain gravesite was maintained properly.

I observed that it wasn't odd at all for Red to want someone to look after Rachel's burial plot, but Rita replied, "That's what's strange, Doc. Rachel was cremated and her ashes scattered." She went on to explain that the gravesite Red mentioned was located in an abandoned cemetery not far from his house. Rita had driven him there several times after his sister, Cora, passed away. Apparently Cora took care of the gravesite up until she got sick the year before. Then she asked Red to take over. To hear Rita describe the place, it was a thicket of brambles, weeds, and broken gravestones, except for a single well-kept plot.

I voiced my curiosity regarding the person buried there. Rita just shook her head and told me she wondered the same thing. When she asked Red, all he said was that the grave was some relative's. According to Rita, Cora had never married, so the person buried in that grave couldn't have been one of her children or an in-law. I cautioned that Cora might have had an illegitimate child, but Rita just shrugged.

Fatigue was getting the best of me, and, knowing a full day at the office awaited me in a few hours, I asked Rita if she was okay with my leaving. Just then the phone rang. We both looked at each other, wondering who might be calling at such a late hour. Rita picked up the receiver, listened for a moment, then motioned for me to take it. "It's Grace, Doc. She needs to speak to you."

Chapter 9

AN ILL TIMED EMERGENCY

The last thing I felt like doing at midnight after attending Red Buchanan's last hours was driving to Richmond, but when Grace phoned with the shocking news that Gray Ashcroft had been involved in a serious automobile accident and needed to be rushed to the MCV Hospital, I knew there was no way I could just head home and go to sleep. Grace told me that Tobias had been notified by Emory, who received the accident report from Sheriff Rogers. Emory informed Tobias that he didn't want some intern or resident taking care of Gray unless Tobias was present to direct things. Tobias agreed to go to Richmond, but insisted on picking up Emory on the way. My partner had the good sense to realize that Emory was in no condition to be driving to the hospital on his own. Tobias asked Grace to track me down and warn me that he might not be back in time for his morning appointments. I promised Grace that I would be in the office at nine to cover for Tobias, but I also let her know I intended to leave for Richmond as soon as I got off the phone.

Grace was not given many details about the accident, only that Gray's car had run off River Road just before a bridge and wound up in the water. According to the sheriff, only the heroic efforts of some Good Samaritan had prevented her from dying at the site. He suspected that the dense fog may have obscured Gray's vision or she swerved to avoid a deer and lost control of her car. Grace had no knowledge of her specific injuries, but obviously Gray was in critical condition.

To this day I vividly recall speeding along Route 5, thinking about the last thing Grace said before hanging up. Apparently Gray had tried to reach me at the office in the late afternoon. Grace let her know that I probably was still at Red Buchanan's. Gray then asked Grace where Red lived, but Grace told her that Red was dying and it would not be a good idea to contact me unless it was an emergency. If Gray had disregarded Grace's advice and tried to find me, she would have needed to drive along River Road to get from Devon to Red's house. Would she have been so desperate to see me that she went out on a foggy evening to the house of a dying man? I cautioned myself against jumping to premature conclusions. It had been a long and emotionally draining day. Any speculation on my part, under the circumstances, was ill-advised. I uttered a silent prayer instead and tried to keep my Jeep under eighty.

Pulling into the Emergency Room driveway, I prepared myself for several possibilities, all of them dreadful. Gray may already have died, or she could be in a coma as a result of serious head injuries. If she had been under water for any period of time, brain damage might have resulted from oxygen deprivation. Should Gray survive, there was a strong likelihood she'd never be the same.

These dark thoughts intermingled with my memory of how stunning she looked when I first visited Devon and she approached from the garden with her champagne flute and basket of flowers. I guiltily recalled her low-cut sundress and how it barely embraced breasts as inviting as down pillows to a bone-weary traveler. The prospect that this earthly testament to womanly perfection might be disfigured nauseated me. I asked the charge nurse where Gray Ashcroft had been taken while fighting back the urge to throw up.

Strange as it sounds, I actually breathed a sigh of relief when the nurse told me Gray had been taken to the Intensive Care Unit. Her condition, of course, was critical, but at least she was alive. I rushed to the ICU, where I found Tobias nervously pacing back and forth in the corridor. When he saw me, he snapped, "Didn't Grace get in touch with you?"

I reminded him that Grace must have contacted me or else I wouldn't be standing next to him at that moment, and I assured him that I planned to cover his morning appointments. Before I could ask about Gray's condition, Tobias grabbed my arm and said, "She's not doing so well, Russell." Tobias rarely made physical contact with anyone. What's more, he almost never called me by my first name. Clearly he was not himself. I suspected that his troubled state involved more than Gray's tragic accident. Tobias hated dealing with the hospital staff. Country docs like him were not accorded much respect at a major medical center like MCV. For his part, Tobias wasn't about to tolerate some wet-behind-the-ears resident telling him what was best for his patient.

I pressed Tobias for details about Gray's accident. He told me she had gone down an embankment into shallow water, and, from the looks of things, hit her head on the steering wheel. She initially lost consciousness, but regained it, according to the EMTs that transported her to the hospital. The attending physician, Dr. Brock, worried that Gray might develop a hematoma, so he had her placed on a monitor to detect any build-up of blood inside her head.

I knew Chandler Brock to be a first-rate ER physician, and I told Tobias that he could be confident Gray would receive excellent care. When he failed to respond to my comment, I realized he hadn't given me all the details. I pressed him for more information, and he grudgingly said that Gray's arms and legs were covered in bruises and her left leg was fractured. Fortunately there were no open wounds, so blood loss was not an issue. Then Tobias paused, as if deciding whether to go on. Finally he revealed that the police indicated Gray must have run off the road at a high speed. The water probably cushioned the impact. Had she struck a tree or a bridge abutment, he added, we would be in the morgue instead of the ICU.

The thought of Gray dying set off my stomach again. I hadn't eaten anything substantial in a long time, which undoubtedly contributed to my queasiness, but I also knew that, if I tried to eat anything, it probably wouldn't stay down. Don't ask me why the prospect of losing Gray Ashcroft affected me the way it did. I certainly was no stranger to death and dying, and I prided myself on being a rational person. No one needed to remind me that mortal existence was precarious and fleeting. All I knew at that moment was that I had feelings for Gray, feelings I could not fully account for. In a matter of several weeks, she had touched a part of me that was dormant for years, despite not having been alone with her for more than a few minutes!

Tobias, in an uncharacteristic gesture, asked me how I was doing. I guess he sensed what was on my mind. I lied and said I was coping, just tired from waiting with Rita until Red Buchanan passed. At the mention of Rita's name, Tobias exclaimed, "The woman's a damn saint. God knows why Lee Buchanan let her go."

Suddenly I realized that Emory was not around. When I asked Tobias, he said Emory was at Gray's bedside, despite hospital rules to the contrary. "I've never seen the man so disconsolate and helpless," Tobias added. "Russell, you've gotten to know him a little. The guy's unflappable. Nothing ever rattles him, until now."

I felt guilty that all my feelings of concern had been concentrated on Gray. Emory was, as Tobias asserted, a remarkable person, but there are limits to what any person can bear.

"Do we know anything about the cause of Gray's accident?" I asked Tobias. "Grace mentioned that the sheriff thought fog might have been a factor."

Tobias nodded and repeated what Grace said, that Gray could have swerved to avoid hitting a deer, over-corrected, and ran off the road. Then he pulled me over to a small alcove off the main corridor and, in a hushed voice, stated what I already was thinking. Gray Ashcroft knew the River Road as well as she knew her own garden, fog or no fog. Why was she out so late? That was the question.

I asked whether Emory had shed any light on the matter. Tobias fumbled around in his coat pocket for his pipe and stuck the unlit pipe in his mouth, complaining about the hospital's rule against smoking. When he told me that Emory admitted having argued with Gray before she left Devon, his voice broke.

Something prompted me to share a hunch with Tobias, though in retrospect I should have kept my mouth shut. "You know what I think?" I whispered. "I think Gray would just as soon leave Devon, and furthermore, I believe she's frustrated with Emory for not accepting the offer from that Richmond lawyer."

Tobias didn't say anything, but appeared to be mulling things over. Finally, he swore me to silence and said that the sheriff had found pieces of a broken bourbon bottle in Gray's car. He went on to point out that Sheriff Rogers had known Gray since they were children, that he was one of Emory's fishing buddies, and that he had no intention of telling anyone about the broken bottle. Tobias then bluntly stated, "And I expect the same from you."

Suddenly I recalled what Grace had said over the phone about someone pulling Gray out of her car. I asked Tobias about it, and he shared that, according to the sheriff, the guy had saved Gray's life. Then he added, "At least for the moment."

I wondered if the Good Samaritan was a local man, but Tobias said Sheriff Rogers never mentioned the individual's name. Apparently his new deputy had been first on the scene and didn't recognize the person. Whoever it was apparently was in a rush to go because by the time Rogers arrived at the scene, the man had left. The deputy reported that the man had been driving along River Road when he approached the Courthouse Creek bridge. He noticed tail lights down by the creek and stopped to investigate. What he found, of course, was Gray's car, nose down in the creek. The car had not plunged into deep water and the engine hadn't conked out. The man managed to get the driver-side door open and carry Gray up the embankment. She was unconscious. Fortunately the man had a two-way radio in his vehicle and called 911.

I considered what Tobias just told me, then asked, "How bad could the fog have been if this guy was able to see two small tail lights down in the creek?"

"What are you suggesting?" Tobias snapped.

Before I could explain, a visibly shaken and exhausted Emory Ashcroft emerged from the ICU. He was too preoccupied and weary to express surprise at my presence. Instead he managed a barely audible "thank you for coming" and reported that there was nothing either of us could do for the moment. Emory suggested we head back home, but Tobias countered with an offer to purchase coffee for us, then apologized for lacking something stronger to add to it. Emory and I went to sit in the waiting room while Tobias headed for the cafeteria. According to Emory, Dr. Brock felt the next twenty-four hours would be critical. If there was no evidence of internal bleeding and Gray remained conscious, the prognosis was reasonably good.

I had never felt at a greater loss for words. Placing my hand on Emory's shoulder, I said, "It's hard to see a loved one in trouble and realize there's absolutely nothing you can do."

Emory's response will forever be etched in my memory because it made me regret what I said. Staring blankly at the closed door to the ICU, he replied, "Being helpless is something I do quite well, Russell."

I was filled with genuine sorrow for Emory. Here was a man who cared deeply for his wife, his home, and his roots, and now he faced the prospect of losing everything. What could I say at a time like this? I opted to ask a question, though I knew before I spoke that it was probably in bad taste.

"Emory, is there any possibility that Gray was upset about your unwillingness to sell Devon?"

Why I said "your unwillingness" I'll never know. Sometimes I'm astounded by my lack of tact. Did I expect Emory to take responsibility for his wife's tragic accident?

Instead of getting angry or acting insulted by my impertinence, which he was more than entitled to do, Emory collected himself and looked at me through bloodshot eyes. His expression conveyed both irony and understanding, as he apparently realized that I cared deeply for him, but that I was in love with his wife. He chose to respond to my question with one of his own. "Are you asking me whether I think Gray tried to take her own life?" I detected a hint of resentment in the query.

I assured Emory that such a thought hadn't crossed my mind, though, of course, it had. Avoiding the truth was something of an art form along the James River. I suspect it goes back to Captain John Smith, who developed a knack for embellishing his exploits. In defense of my falsehood, I noted the broken bourbon bottle and observed that individuals who are upset often turn to alcohol for relief.

"There's no substitute for history, my friend," Emory responded in a voice so calm I thought he might be mocking me. "You are right about one thing, Gray was upset. But it had nothing to do with my reaction to Brown's offer to buy Devon."

I debated whether to probe deeper into what were clearly the private affairs of the Ashcrofts. My curiosity got the better of me and I inquired about what was bothering Gray. Emory chuckled and asked if I had a license to practice psychiatry. It was good to see him relax a little. "Russell, the plain fact of the matter is that my wonderful wife would never forgive me, in this world or the next, if I sold Devon."

How could I have been so far off the mark? I admitted being totally confused, and Emory replied that my confusion was completely understandable. "You would have had to know Gray when she was a young woman of modest means loaded to the water line with dreams. All kinds of dreams. Dreams of being a lady, someone of significance. Devon enabled her to live her dreams."

Why had Emory shared this insight with me, I wondered. Was he admitting that Gray had married him for reasons other than love? If so, I failed to detect any note of bitterness or resentment in his voice.

Emory continued, "The sad fact, Russell, is that my wife could never live anywhere but Devon. She has become as much a part of the legacy as I am. More so, I suspect." Emory told me that the previous day he decided that Devon either had to be sold to Brown or put on the market. The coffers were virtually empty, and he didn't want the bank to take over. When he informed Gray of his decision, she flew into a rage, yelling at him, telling him he was a failure, attacking him for spending more time on his various history projects than on managing the farm.

Try as I might, I could not imagine Gray Ashcroft conducting herself in this way. Had Emory contrived this story with some ulterior motive in mind? No sooner was this question raised than I chided myself for once again considering unwarranted possibilities. I asked Emory how he responded to Gray's outburst.

Emory admitted trying to defuse Gray's anger by reminding her of the enormous burden that would be lifted from their shoulders if they no longer had to worry about maintaining Devon and all the property surrounding it. Then he put a question to her: "Wouldn't it be exciting for you and me to start a new life together?" Gray's response was terse and tinged with bitterness. If Emory wanted to start a new life, he could do it on his own. She turned and ran out of the mansion, got into her car, and drove away. That was the last Emory saw of her until he arrived at the hospital in Richmond.

At the time I recall thinking, Why do we always want what we can't have? Are we cursed with some gene that predisposes us to dissatisfaction? All Emory ever wanted was to study history. All Gray ever wanted was to live out her days as the mistress of Devon. All Red Buchanan ever wanted was to take people hunting and fishing. All Rita desired was Lee. Do we consciously seek the things we know we can't have? Is it all part of some grand scheme to ensure that good folks die disappointed? And what about me, I wondered? What did I crave that I couldn't have? The answer was painfully clear. She was lying in the ICU, lingering between existence and the void.

Emory asked me what he had said to stop the conversation. For some odd reason, I wanted to share my unspoken thoughts, but I decided against doing so. Instead, I asked him if he believed that Gray had intended to take her own life when she rushed off.

"There's not a doubt in my mind," Emory asserted. "You know, it's ironic in a way. For a time, I actually mulled over the benefits of suicide. If I made it look like an accident, Gray could collect the life insurance money and keep Devon afloat."

When Emory said this, my fondness for the man increased tenfold. I replied, "You really love Gray, don't you?"

Tears welled up in Emory's eyes and he slumped a bit, placing his hands on his knees. When he straightened up, I detected a faint smile on his lips. There was only one problem with his scheme, Emory revealed. His life insurance lapsed because he no longer could afford the payments. Gray didn't know because he was too embarrassed to tell her.

I chuckled and said his case was one instance when poverty turned out to be a blessing. Looking down the corridor, I saw Tobias struggling to balance three cups of hot coffee. Before he came within earshot, I posed one more question. "How can you be so certain Gray intended to kill herself?"

Emory responded without looking at me. "Because the sheriff informed me there were no skid marks at the point where Gray's car left the road. She made no effort to stop, Russell"

Chapter 10

WAITING

I had the good sense not to drive back to Charles City County from the hospital until I got a little rest. Tobias and I stretched out on two lumpy couches in the waiting room, while Emory periodically poked his head in the ICU to check on Gray's condition. He expressed frustration over the ICU staff's refusal to let him remain at her bedside, but understood he might be in the way and a possible carrier of germs.

The events of the past two days clearly took their toll on me. I had not felt so bone-weary and sleep-deprived since my days as a resident. The irony that the setting in each case was the same did not escape me. A deep, restoring sleep, of course, was impossible under present circumstances, what with my concern for Gray and the ambulance sirens that periodically punctuated the evening calm. I managed to rest my eyes for a few hours, but my mind refused to shut down. When the next shift of nurses arrived at seven, I rose and went to the restroom, splashed some water on my face, and told Tobias I'd be heading back to the office after I grabbed a bite to eat.

The hospital cafeteria was just as depressing as it had been when I was a resident. Looking around at the heavy-lidded, unshaven docs clutching their coffee cups as if they were sacred chalices reminded me of the countless mornings when I stumbled down to the cafeteria after a night of fun and games with the Grim Reaper. I recalled the bizarre thoughts that frequently accompanied sleep deprivation. One morning I asked the chief resident sitting across from me if he regretted going into medicine. He forced a wry smile and said no, but he sure as hell regretted choosing to sit across from me. Another morning after having tried to patch up victims of a three-car accident, I tried to organize my cafeteria mates into a chorus to sing the Mickey Mouse Club song. Many mornings I fell sound asleep over my breakfast, only to awake with a start when I was paged over the intercom.

True to form, this morning I again drifted off in the cafeteria because I remember daydreaming something distressing. The gist of it was that my life was nothing more than an assortment of random memories. The image came to mind of a broken necklace, costume jewels and a few pearls scattered across a table with no chain to hold them together. I snapped out of it when a nurse asked if I was ill.

The sun had risen over Church Hill as I drove east on Broad Street toward home. Had it been night time, I would not have felt comfortable in this part of the city, but even the most dangerous neighborhoods can seem benign in the early morning. Rather than hop on the Interstate, I decided to take the long way home, a route that took me out Williamsburg Road past Sandston and the airport. It wasn't that this choice was more scenic. Far from it. But I had no desire to return to the office by the quickest possible route. I had some thinking to do.

Once I reached Bottoms Bridge, I turned south on the Elko Road. This neck of the woods had swarmed with rebels and bluecoats in the summer of 1862. Emory had schooled me on McClellan's ill-fated campaign to take Richmond with his tales of Lee replacing Johnston as Confederate commander and Stonewall Jackson's uncharacteristic lack of leadership during the Seven Days. My thoughts during the morning drive, however, were not about the Civil War. I considered what Emory suggested the night before, that Gray had tried to take her own life. It was upsetting to think that this woman whom I barely knew, but with whom I was so infatuated, was so fragile that the prospect of leaving Devon drove her to self-destruction.

By the time I reached Route 5, my concern for Gray had morphed into self-pity. Was I really such a lousy judge of female character? My marriage to Mary Beth could be explained as youthful impetuousness, the triumph of hope over reality. My attraction to Gray Ashcroft was a different matter entirely. I should have been able to spot the symptoms of destructive ambition by that time. No wonder I lived a monk's life. It probably was for the best.

Then I thought about Rita, her compassion for Red and patient devotion to his son. Though she never admitted to me that she still waited for Lee to resolve his issues, I had no doubt that Rita resisted the advances of potential suitors because she expected Lee eventually would come to his senses and ask for her hand. Why, I wondered, couldn't I have found such a loyal and loving companion?

As I neared the turn-off for Red's house, I decided to drop by and see if Rita was still there and if the undertaker had picked up Red's body. I planned to call Grace from Red's and tell her I'd be arriving shortly. As I drove up to the house, I noticed a pickup truck parked next to Rita's Buick. At first I thought Jess Tucker's hearse might be in the shop and he had brought the truck instead. Then I spotted the Florida tags on the truck.

Rita came to the door and said she was glad to see me. Her moist eyes told me she had been crying. Rita gestured toward the bed where Red still lay. Beside him in the shadows sat a man I assumed was Lee, head in hands. "He arrived an hour ago," Rita whispered as she motioned for me to join her on the porch. "He just sits there saying 'I'm sorry' and staring. I don't know what to do, Doc."

I asked Rita if she had notified Jess Tucker about picking up the body. She shook her head and explained that Lee first needed some time with his father.

I thought about Red's passing, then about my own eventual homegoing. Which was worse, I thought, having your only kin show up too late to say goodbye or not having any kin at all to mourn your death?

"You know why Lee didn't make it in time?" Rita asked. I shook my head. "He stopped to help Gray Ashcroft. He was on his way here when he saw her taillights reflecting off the water over by the Courthouse. She must have just run off the road. Lee waded into the creek and pulled her out of the car. She was unconscious. It's a blessing the car came to rest in shallow water."

I'm not a religious man, but at times I find myself asking, "Was it meant to be?" This was one of those times. Here was an estranged son rushing home to see his dying father and he stops to save a woman who might have been trying to kill herself. Being a Good Samaritan prevented him from saying goodbye to Red. What perverse God would mean for such a bittersweet string of events to transpire?

I asked Rita why Lee hadn't come straight to Red's after rescuing Gray. She explained that he was a mess, his clothes were soaked and muddy. The deputy gave Lee directions to his house and told him to get cleaned up before going to see his father. Lee was so exhausted after his drive from Florida and his efforts to pull Gray from her vehicle that he fell sound asleep on the deputy's sofa. When he awoke, he drove straight to Red's, but of course it was too late.

"I feel so badly for Lee," Rita said. "Here he was trying to make things right."

Lee spoke up from the parlor. "And once again I fucked up."

I turned and saw Lee rising from his seat by the bed. His sand-colored hair was a mess, and he bore his father's squared jaw and broad forehead. If I hadn't known he was in his early forties, I would have taken him to be ten years younger. Given his muscular build and deep tan, it wasn't hard to see why Rita was attracted to Lee. "I'm Doc Curry," I announced, extending my hand as Lee joined us on the porch. "I'm sorry about your dad."

Lee told me he was grateful I had done what I could to make Red's last hours comfortable. Then he added, "I just wish it had been me, not you, at his bedside when he passed."

Rita clutched Lee's hand. "You did the best you could, darling."

Lee looked away and wiped his eyes. "Here I finally grow up enough to realize that it's not all about me and that I've got to stop feeling sorry for myself, and look what happens. I get another reason to feel sorry for myself. Now I'm a god-damned orphan!"

Rita suggested we get some coffee and sit on the porch. As we watched the fog slowly burn off, Lee reminisced about how he and his dad used to go fishing before the sun came up. Rita tried to coax Biscuit and Gravy to join us, but they insisted on standing guard by Red's bedside. I grew concerned about getting to the office to handle Tobias's appointments, but I understood that Lee needed to vent. He talked about life at home being so laid back and how Red was too easy-going and lacking in ambition. After his mother died, Lee began to resent Red's ways and worry that he might be susceptible to following in his father's footsteps if he hung around any longer. Lee also came to believe that his mother deserved better than she got from Red. He started having nightmares about becoming another "backwoods Bubba", as he referred to his father. The more anxious Lee grew, the more he argued with Red. Red just listened, never losing his temper, which upset Lee even more. Eventually Lee decided that the only way he could make something of himself was to get as far away from home as possible.

As Lee spoke, I couldn't help thinking about Rita. What must have been going through her head as she listened to the man she loved discuss his life without ever mentioning her? Was she so insignificant that it never crossed Lee's mind to consider her feelings or how his leaving might affect her? Recalling what Red had told me about why Lee left, I suspected the story I was getting had been sanitized, but I declined to probe any deeper. Whatever emotional energy I could muster at the time was focused on Gray Ashcroft.

I tuned out Lee as I considered what I needed to do for Gray. If she were going to die, I wanted to be at her bedside, so I decided to return to the hospital after office hours. Then I apologized for needing to leave and drove to the office. On the way I wondered whether Lee had come back to stay and, if so, whether he intended to work things out with Rita.

When I arrived at the office, the waiting room was full. Spring in the Virginia Piedmont means a profusion of growing things, and growing things, in turn, mean allergy problems. Since I had to see Tobias's patients as well as my own, I didn't get a break all day. Grace did her best to keep waiting patients entertained. News of Gray's accident and Lee's courageous effort to save her had spread like gossip in a hair salon, and every time I came out of the examining room, I saw several patients huddled around Grace for details. She was obviously in her glory.

Tobias returned in the late afternoon and told me that Gray was having longer spells when she was lucid, but she continued to experience considerable pain. Dr. Brock was reluctant to give her strong painkillers for fear they might mask other symptoms related to her head injury. Gray needed to be kept under constant surveillance for at least two or three more days. I asked how Emory was holding up, and Tobias said he was physically and emotionally spent. He insisted that Emory go home and get some rest. Emory reluctantly agreed, but only because he wished to thank Lee Buchanan personally for saving Gray. It pleased me to think that I might be alone with Gray when I went to visit her that evening.

With Tobias back in the office, the remaining patients were seen by dinner time. He planned to return to the hospital after he cleaned up and ate dinner. I didn't tell him that I intended to visit her as soon as I left the office. Tobias knew, of course, that I was smitten, so I didn't need to invite a sermon on the sanctity of marriage and the foolishness of infatuation for a man my age. Tobias, I should add, was no saint. He enjoyed many manly vices, including off-color jokes, strong liquor, gambling, and big cigars, but he drew the line at coveting thy neighbor's wife. I, on the other hand, had no idea where I drew the line.

On the drive to Richmond, I stopped at a roadside barbecue joint for a bite to eat. Having had nothing substantial since my brief breakfast in the hospital cafeteria, I was feeling lightheaded and realized I required some nourishment before visiting Gray. I arrived at the hospital around seven and lied to the ICU nurse in order to see Gray. Dr. Brock ordered that Gray was to have no visitors except her husband and Tobias. I told the nurse that I was Tobias's partner and that he asked me to stop by and check on how Gray was doing. There was no doubt in my mind that I would receive a stern lecture when Tobias learned of my deception.

Gray was sleeping when I entered the ICU, so I reviewed her chart at the foot of the bed and sat down to wait. I guessed it would take Tobias at least an hour to shower, change clothes, and eat dinner. Then another forty-five minutes to drive to the hospital and park. If I left the hospital by eight, our paths wouldn't cross. Watching Gray's labored breathing, I wondered how I would feel if she were my wife. Having a relationship invited vulnerability. I had invested myself in a woman once before and paid a stiff price. My depleted savings, I knew, were unprepared for a new withdrawal. What was it about Gray Ashcroft that attracted me in spite of my better judgment? Initially it had been nothing more than her voice over the phone, that voice without any trace of harshness or hesitation, a voice expertly tuned for candlelit dinners and playful intimacy, a voice capable of erasing a day's dreary demands with a single greeting.

"Russell, is that really you, or am I dreaming?" It was as if Gray had intuited my thoughts.

"We're all very worried about you," I responded. Why had I said "we're all very worried"? Why didn't I just come out and admit that I was worried about her?

Despite the IV taped to her arm, Gray reached over and placed her hand on mine. "It was sweet of you to come. Emory told me that you also were here last night."

I gently squeezed her hand. I knew what I wanted to say, but I held back because I feared that revealing my feelings might cause unwanted confusion. Instead, I said, "Your chart shows improvement. You're definitely a fighter."

Gray closed her eyes and her forehead tightened as she experienced a jolt of pain.

"Are you all right? Should I call the nurse?"

She shook her head.

"Do you remember anything about the accident?"

Gray's eyes slowly opened, and she looked at me, seemingly seeking a signal to proceed. "Russell, I'm going to tell you something, something that as long as I'm alive you must not share with anyone, not Emory, not Tobias, not anyone. Do I have your word as a gentleman?"

I knew what she was going to tell me, but why she felt the need to do so puzzled me. Obviously Emory had not confronted Gray with the fact that she had been drinking and that she had left no skid marks before plunging into the creek. I also realized that he never would. Nor would Gray, I now suspected, disclose the truth to her husband. It appeared that honesty was not the bedrock on which the Ashcrofts' relationship was built. Could it be, I wondered, that knowing everything about one's mate was not essential for a strong marriage? One thing was certain. Gray and Emory loved each other deeply.

"You have my word, Gray."

"My accident, Russell, was no accident."

Perhaps I failed to register sufficient surprise at her revelation because Gray paused and looked at me in a curious way. I sensed she was waiting for me to say something.

"I find it hard to believe that you would do anything to harm yourself."

"I can't bear it any longer," Gray cried. "It pains me to think of Emory having to sell Devon. Devon is who he is, Russell. You know that. You've heard him tell stories about his ancestors. He loves being a part of Ashcroft history. What in God's name would he do if Devon were sold?"

Gray's remarks caught me by surprise. They reflected no trace of self-pity or personal concern about leaving Devon. If she had tried to kill herself, it clearly wasn't for selfish reasons.

"Tell me, Gray, how would Emory be better off without you? Surely you know he loves you more than a piece of real estate."

Gray tried to change position without dislodging the IV tube. I could tell she was uncomfortable. After a moment she looked away and said, "If you loved someone a great deal, wouldn't you try to do anything you could to help them?"

I nodded without grasping where she was headed.

"I thought that if I died in an accident, Emory could collect on my life insurance and not be forced to sell Devon."

"You can't be serious." I didn't have the heart to tell her that Emory had failed to keep up the life insurance payments for Gray and himself.

"I really do love that man, Russell."

A wave of admiration and regret swept over me, momentarily rendering me speechless. I could not imagine anyone loving me enough to take their own life, nor could I imagine loving anyone so much that I would consider the same. No one, that is, with the possible exception of the woman whose pale blue eyes I was trying to avoid. "Why are you telling me this, Gray?" Tears formed in my eyes.

"Because I know, Russell."

"You know?"

"I know why you're here now and why you came earlier."

"So you know how I feel about you?"

"I've known since your first visit to Devon."

Was I that transparent? I felt like my private diary had just appeared in the Times-Dispatch. Whatever equilibrium I thought existed between Gray and me vanished. I now understood that a one-way mirror separated the two of us, permitting Gray to glimpse my innermost feelings, but denying me a view of hers.

"I can see I've upset you, Russell. I'm getting pretty good at disturbing those I care about."

"Can I just ask you one question?"

She nodded.

"Did you try to reach me the night of the accident?"

Suddenly a familiar voice intruded. "Well, this is a surprise! Two surprises in fact."

I turned to see Tobias approaching with a nurse.

"I'm surprised to find my favorite patient awake, and I'm surprised to find you here, Dr. Curry."

I felt like a high school student who had just been caught without a hall pass by the principal.

Chapter **11**

DUST TO WATER

Gray continued to improve and was released from the hospital on Friday. I did not visit her after our Tuesday evening conversation at the hospital. It wasn't that I worried about what people, particularly Tobias, would say. In the best tradition of my Virginia ancestors, I simply came to the realization that Gray Ashcroft was a lost cause. To this day I remain unsure of what I actually thought might transpire between us. After we talked at the hospital, though, I understood Gray would never leave Emory.

Tobias never said a word about finding me at Gray's bedside, but I sensed afterwards that he regarded me differently. No longer did he poke his head in my office to see how things were going. When we did speak, the topic was strictly medical business. I was uncertain if Emory ever found out from Tobias that I had revisited Gray.

Gray returned to Devon with orders from Dr. Brock to get as much rest as possible for the next month and avoid any strenuous activity. She was not to garden, lift anything heavier than a glass of bourbon, or drive. The fractured left leg had been immobilized in a cast, and Gray was warned against bearing any weight on it until the cast came off. When she needed to move about, crutches or a walker were required. Once the cast was removed, Gray was supposed to work with a physical therapist to strengthen her muscles.

When Emory went to thank Lee Buchanan for saving Gray's life, he ran into Rita and asked if she would be willing to help care for Gray during her convalescence. I knew that he could not afford to hire her, but I also knew he would not feel comfortable leaving Gray with only Edward to help her if she needed assistance.

Lee Buchanan stopped by the office on the Friday Gray was discharged and asked Grace if he could speak with me. When Grace entered the treatment room, I was examining Billy Parker. She apologized for interrupting and explained that Lee was in the waiting room wishing to see me, then added that once again he was being hailed as a local hero thanks to his efforts to rescue Gray. Rita already had told me about his decorations from the Korean conflict. Now, according to Grace, some people wanted to nominate Lee for Charles City County's Citizen of the Year award.

I finished cleaning the gravel bits out of the wound Billy Parker received when he fell off his bike and went to my office, where Lee was waiting. He thanked me again for easing his father's suffering and informed me that Red's ashes were delivered from the crematorium in Richmond. Since I had been at Red's bedside when he passed, Lee and Rita wanted me to accompany them when they cast his remains on the River. They planned to go out the next day, Saturday, if it didn't rain. I told Lee his father was, in my estimation, a decent and loving man and that I'd be honored to accompany them.

Lee and Rita arrived at my house a little after seven the next morning. An early start was required in order to beat the rain moving up from the south. Rita poured me a cup of strong coffee from her thermos and handed it to me along with a container of doughnuts. It pleased me to see that Lee and Rita were getting along well. We left my house and headed toward Devon. Emory had graciously agreed to let us use his boat, telling Rita that he would be forever in Lee's debt.

When we arrived at the plantation, Emory came out and greeted us warmly, then escorted us down to the dock. I inquired about Gray's recuperation, and he replied that she was very glad to be back home. Dr. Brock felt that the risk of a subdural hemorrhage at this point was slight. Gray just needed to be patient while her body healed. I considered suggesting that Gray might benefit from seeing a psychiatrist, but doing so in front of Rita and Lee clearly was inappropriate.

As we walked toward the River, Emory tugged at my elbow to slow my progress. He whispered something about a phone call and wanting to talk with me when I had a free moment.

When we reached Emory's boat, he picked up an extra can of gasoline and handed it to me, winking as he said, "Just in case." The memory of the evening Gray and I waited anxiously for Emory to return from his outing on the River made me tremble. Though the incident only occurred a few weeks earlier, so much had happened in the interim that it seemed like months had passed.

Emory spoke with Lee for a few minutes about the currents in that part of the River, then untied the boat and we were off. Lee steered the boat eastward as Emory grew smaller on the dock. I felt pangs of guilt for having made no effort to support him since Gray was hospitalized. I also wondered about the mysterious phone call Emory mentioned and why he needed to talk with me about it.

No one said anything for a while. The serenity of the River in the morning offered respite from recent events, and each of us seemed ready to take advantage of it. I imagined Lee might be thinking about whatever had really caused him to abandon his father. Rita probably was considering the prospect of getting back together with Lee. For my part, I reflected on Gray and what the future might hold for her. No longer was there any possibility I would be part of that future. The unspoken farewell to my fantasy was accompanied by an odd mixture of regret and relief.

As we motored pass Sturgeon Point, Rita broke the silence by asking Lee where he intended to scatter Red's ashes.

"I was thinking of just past Dancing Point, where the Chickahominy runs into the James. Dad loved to fish there."

Rita responded that she didn't care for that location. According to her, locals believed Dancing Point was haunted by evil spirits. "Besides," she added, "if you'd spent more time with your father, you'd know he hadn't fished the James in years. It's too polluted. He hated what had been done to the River."

"So where would the captain suggest we scatter Dad's ashes?" Lee shot back with more than a tinge of irritation. I held my breath, hoping a squabble would not ensue.

"If you're really interested in my opinion, and it doesn't sound like you are," Rita replied, "I think Red would rest more comfortably if we took him a ways up the Chickahominy. It needn't be too far."

I braced myself for what I was certain would be Lee's response.

"So you think his ashes will just settle to the bottom where they're scattered and not float downstream to the James?" Lee snickered.

"Oh, do what you want, Lee. You always have." Rita looked away in dismay.

"What's that supposed to mean, Rita?"

"Never mind." Rita looked at me, hopeful that I would intervene.

Lee's jaw relaxed a little. "I'm sorry, Rita. I shouldn't have said what I did. You knew my dad better than I did, and you were around when I wasn't there to help. I think you're right. He'd feel more at home on the Chickahominy."

Rita took a deep breath and nodded.

Lee commenced to reminiscing, observing how his father had tried to teach him to appreciate the woods and waterways. Red's waxing poetic about the tranquil delights of nature failed, however, to impress young Lee. He just believed his father was out of touch with the world. Lee grew more sad with each memory he shared.

Rita shifted closer to Lee and put her hand on his shoulder.

"All he ever really wanted in life," Lee continued, "besides being close to Mom, was time to hunt and fish."

Lee throttled down, cutting the buzz of the motor to a low murmur. Then he looked at me. "Doc, do you believe in fate?"

"Why do you ask?" I responded.

"I was just thinking about Dad."

"I'm no expert on such matters, Lee, but it seems to me fate's a lot like this River. It carries you along for a while, deposits you somewhere, and then it's up to you."

Lee didn't reply.

Rita asked Lee what he thought fate had in store for him.

"I've been wondering about that a lot, Rita." It was the first time I heard him refer to Rita by name. "I'm thinking I was meant to live right here along the James, not down in Florida."

Rita's shoulders seemed to rise along with her head when he said this.

Nothing more was said until we reached Dancing Point. In the distance downstream I made out what I thought to be Jamestown Island. Lee rounded the point and headed up the Chickahominy as Rita explained why people believed the area was haunted. A man named Lightfoot owned a plantation at Dancing Point, and he wanted to drain the marshy land around the confluence of the two rivers so it could be cultivated. Apparently, for unknown reasons, the Devil opposed the plan. Lightfoot and the Old Deluder decided to have a dancing contest to determine whether the project would proceed. Lightfoot out-danced the Devil and drained the marshes, but nothing worthwhile was ever able to grow on the salvaged land. Locals swore they saw fires at night on the point and ghostly figures dancing around them.

After ten minutes of cruising upriver, Lee cut the motor and took the urn containing Red's ashes from Rita. In a soft voice, he said, "Dad, you never pretended to be more than you were, and what you were was a decent, hard-working, God-fearing man, a good husband, and a tolerant father." Then he removed the top from the urn and added, "I'm sorry I didn't appreciate you the way I should have." Rita burst into tears, and I wiped my eyes.

As Lee waved the open urn over the water, I couldn't help wondering what it was about fathers and sons. Why did sons find it so hard to understand their fathers? If I have achieved any stature in this world, it is because I wanted my father to be proud of me, but if I'm totally honest, I can't say I was very proud of my father. He sold some kind of insurance and bragged a lot about selling customers policies they didn't need. In elementary school, I always hated to share what my father did for a living when the teacher went around the room asking students. Back in those days, teachers never asked what mothers did. Everyone knew mothers stayed home and took care of their families. It always seemed I had to follow some kid whose father was a store owner or a builder or a military officer. I didn't really know what insurance was or why anyone needed it. When my father passed away, I was at his bedside. He took my hand and told me how proud he was of me and the fine doctor I had become. I wanted desperately to say I was proud of him as well, but I couldn't manage to do it. I've never forgiven myself.

Drying her eyes with a handkerchief, Rita declared, "Now Red and Rachel are together again."

"Maybe in heaven," Lee said with a chuckle, "but not here. Mom insisted her ashes be spread on her garden. Plants need rich fertilizer, she said."

"Eventually the land and the water become one," Rita added

The return trip afforded some lovely views of Evelynton Plantation on the north shore and Flowerdew Hundred on the south shore. At one time only Berkeley and Shirley were open to the public, but to make ends meet other plantation owners along the River began to admit visitors at certain times of the year. During Garden Week last April I never saw so many out-of-state drivers along Route 5. It was unfortunate Emory and Gray had not considered converting Devon into an historic attraction long ago. They might have managed to keep the books balanced if they did.

When we got back to Devon, Emory was driving golf balls into the River. I saw Gray up on the terrace, sunning herself and reading. Emory laid his golf club down and walked over to help secure the boat to the dock. I handed him the unused canister of gasoline, remarking that we apparently had more success conserving fuel than he had. Emory smiled and asked Rita and Lee to stop by the terrace to see Gray. I imagined she wished to thank Lee for saving her life.

As we walked up the lawn, Emory once again drew me aside. "That phone call I told you about," he whispered. "It was a lawyer for Commonwealth Power. He heard I might be interested in selling."

"You think Brown told him?" I asked.

"I doubt it. Why would he want competitors, especially Commonwealth Power? More likely it was that lawyer of his who spilled the beans. I didn't get a good feeling about him."

I asked if the lawyer from Commonwealth Power tendered an offer.

Emory shook his head, then indicated the huge corporation was prepared to convert the Ashcroft estate into a major development, including a golf course and high-end homes. Just before we reached the terrace, Emory added, "Russell, I'm as indecisive as a squirrel trying to cross a busy road. Please let me know what you'd do if you were in my shoes."

I said I'd think about it, then went over to where Gray was sitting. "Why Mrs. Ashcroft, you look so much better than the last time I saw you." Dropping the formality, I added, "It's wonderful to see you back where you belong." I instantly regretted adding "where you belong". Life for the Ashcrofts was challenging enough without my thoughtless comments.

Gray motioned for Lee to come closer. "You, sir, are my knight. What you did was very heroic."

It was obvious that words did not come easily to Lee. He had not expected to meet Gray when he came to borrow Emory's boat and therefore had given no thought to what he might say to her. "Mr. Ashcroft already thanked me, ma'am."

"I know he did, Mr. Buchanan, but you need to hear it straight from the mare's mouth, as it were."

Lee blushed and looked away.

"By saving my life you were unable to reach your dear father before he passed. That was a terrible sacrifice, and I wanted you to know how grateful I am."

"I suspect Dad would have wanted me to do what I did. I'm just glad I was at the right place at the right time. If I hadn't seen your headlights in the water...." Lee didn't finish his sentence. Playing the role of hero clearly stretched him to the limits of his social skills.

Gray asked me to reach down beside her chair and pick up an object that had some weight to it. The sun struck the silver loving cup, sending a blinding reflection toward Lee and Rita. "Emory and I want you to have this as a very, very small token of our appreciation. It has been in the family for over two hundred years." She pointed to the Ashcroft family crest engraved on the side of the cup.

"You don't have to do this, Mrs. Ashcroft."

"I know, Lee. I only wish I could do more."

To prevent a meaningful moment from becoming awkward, I suggested that Gray might need some rest. I also lied and claimed there were several patients I needed to see. Rita told Gray she would come on Monday to help out. Emory then walked us to Rita's car and thanked Lee again. He shook my hand and told me he'd keep in touch.

Lee handed the loving cup to Rita and got behind the steering wheel. She remarked how beautiful it was. As we drove off, I explained that Emory told me earlier about the tradition surrounding the loving cup. In bygone days the Ashcrofts hosted big parties for some of Virginia's most illustrious citizens. To get people in a gay mood, several loving cups were filled with champagne, crème de menthe, and ice. The cups were passed from guest to guest, each holding on to both handles and taking a drink. The challenge was to take the last drink and sufficiently empty the vessel so that no drops came out when the loving cup was turned upside down. If only one drop fell, the unsuccessful guest had to sing a song for everyone. If no drop fell, the guest got to pick someone else to sing.

"Sounds like an excellent way to get a lot of people drunk very quickly," Lee exclaimed. I agreed.

"You know, I'm sure I've seen the Ashcroft family crest somewhere," Rita said, studying the engraving on the loving cup.

I suggested she might have seen the crest in a museum. Rita shook her head and insisted she had seen it recently. As Lee pulled out onto Route 5, she asked me if I'd mind making one stop before being dropped off at the office. I confessed there really were no patients for me to see and that I simply needed an excuse to leave the Ashcrofts. Rita poked me in the ribs and asked whether I had a heavy date that night. She instructed Lee to drive past Adkins Store and take the first road on the left.

"The Wild Turkey Road?" he asked.

She nodded and explained that there was an abandoned cemetery she needed to visit. "I promised your father, Lee, that I'd make sure a particular grave site was kept clear of weeds and briars and such. Do you have any idea who's buried there?"

Lee said he didn't recall a name, but he had heard that his aunt Cora used to drop by Red's once or twice a year after visiting some overgrown cemetery. Cora lived in West Point near the big paper mill. She died a few weeks after Lee went to Florida.

Rita put her hand on Lee's knee. "You know your dad was very upset that you didn't come back for Cora's funeral." I sensed Lee was about to respond, but changed his mind. Rita went on to say that every family seemed to have its secrets. "We think we know all there is to know about our kin until one day we discover that some uncle was a pedophile or a father had a mistress in the next town."

Lee muttered something about glass houses.

When Lee turned at the Wild Turkey Road, I realized I was in an area that was new to me. In those days I made house calls and thought I had seen just about every part of Charles City County. After a quarter mile the pavement ran out. More accurately, it just seemed to melt into dirt. The absence of deep ruts in the spring suggested that the road was lightly traveled. We passed an occasional side road thick with vegetation and several abandoned farms, but no visible evidence that people inhabited this area. I joked that the road probably got its name because wild turkeys were the only residents. Lee noted that this section of the county used to be populated by poor black farmers. Most of them had left for better opportunities decades earlier. After a few miles Rita told Lee to pull the car off to the side of a clearing. What looked at first like a former pasture that nature had reclaimed turned out to be an old burying ground. Traces of an iron fence formed a rough rectangle about 50 by 100 yards.

It wasn't difficult to spot the gravesite that Red asked Rita to tend. Everything else was a mass of waist-high weeds, brambles, scrub locust, and blackberry vines. We gingerly made our way through the thicket, trying to avoid snaring our clothes. Rita fretted she might step on a snake, but when Lee offered to hold her hand, she declined. Upon reaching our destination, it was obvious that considerable time had passed since Red last came to clear away underbrush. The simple stone marking the grave bore a brief inscription:

AM

THE LORD GIVETH AND THE LORD TAKETH

1874

As we set to work pulling weeds and rerouting blackberry vines, Rita speculated on the inscription. She thought "AM" must have been an infant or stillborn birth. In these parts it wasn't unusual for only the Christian name to be used in such cases. I heard Rita's voice break as she said, "How sad to think of this little one out here all alone." Her comment brought tears to my eyes.

"I'll bet AM's parents are around here somewhere," Lee called out as he wandered off. "Who'd just bury a baby in the middle of nowhere?"

"Someone who didn't want anyone to know about it," Rita responded.

I suggested that we clear away some of the vegetation from the area adjacent to AM's marker. The space immediately to the right contained no mounds or gravestones, but when we shifted to the left side and tore out the underbrush, two adjacent mounds were revealed. Both bore markers, each less weathered than AM's. The stone nearest to AM's read:

Sarah Profitt
1849-1900

The stone to the left of Sarah Profitt's read:

Solomon Profitt
Died 1904

Rita asked Lee if the Profitts could have been related to his mother's people, but he claimed all of Rachel Buchanan's relatives lived in North Carolina. Rita added that Red's sister, Cora, was buried in West Point and had never married. Suddenly I recalled where I had heard the name, Solomon Profitt.

"You know, I met a man at the Ashcrofts' place who said his great grandfather's name was Solomon Profitt. He'd been enslaved at Devon."

Rita stared at me in amazement. "Don't tell me the Ashcrofts were entertaining a black person."

I felt it wasn't my place to share the reason why Henry Brown had come to Devon, so I simply indicated the man had some business related to the farm. Both Rita and Lee looked at me suspiciously. I guess my skills at stretching the truth need some work.

"If this Solomon Profitt is the same person, that would mean this is a Negro cemetery," Lee said in astonishment. "Why would my aunt and my father have taken care of a gravesite in a Negro cemetery?"

"And why would your father have felt that keeping the plot cleared was so important that he asked me on his deathbed to take over?" Rita asked.

"Hold on," I interjected. "We're jumping to conclusions.

There could be other Solomon Profitts. Didn't some former slaves adopt the names of their former owners?" I took out a handkerchief and dabbed at several places on my arms where brambles had torn open my skin. "I know just the person to help solve this mystery. Emory Ashcroft has been studying local cemeteries for years."

Chapter **12**

A MATTER OF GRAVE CONCERN

The following day, Sunday, I drove over to the Ashcrofts. At the time I remember thinking how much the axis around which my life rotated had shifted toward the River, and more specifically toward Devon. There I was, recovering from a foolish fantasy over Gray Ashcroft while I served as her husband's confidant. My list of Ashcroft-related responsibilities was growing faster than kudzu. In his latest request, Emory sought my advice regarding the Commonwealth Power proposal. That Sunday, however, I arrived at Devon with a request of my own. Did Emory know anything about the cemetery where Solomon and Sarah Profitt and the mysterious "AM" were buried? I also planned to explain to Gray why thus far I had avoided paying her a social call during her convalescence. As I bounced along the deteriorating driveway, however, I didn't have a clue about what I would offer as my excuse.

After knocking repeatedly, I was about to leave when Edward opened the door. He said that Mr. Ashcroft was taking a phone call in the study and that Mrs. Ashcroft was resting. Edward motioned for me to follow him out to the terrace behind the mansion. Rita sat at the far end facing the River, obviously enjoying some quiet reverie. I decided not to disturb her, but the slamming of the screen door as Edward re-entered the mansion startled her and she pivoted toward the noise. As soon as she saw me, she stood up and burst into tears. My physician's training prompted me to seek the source of her distress, but my instincts told me to forgo inquiry and offer a consoling hug instead. I must admit that, despite the circumstances, the warmth of Rita's body against my own generated a pleasing mixture of re-assurance and stimulation. Rita was the first to speak.

"Forgive me, Doc. You deserve a better greeting."

I offered her my handkerchief. "What's wrong, Rita? Is it Mrs. Ashcroft?" Once I uttered her name, my anxiety level rose. Had Gray taken a sudden turn for the worse? My heart began to race, and I wondered if Rita, whose head remained pressed against my shoulder, detected my quickened pulse.

"No, no, it's not Mrs. Ashcroft. It's silly old me, Doc." Rita pulled away and straightened up, still dabbing the corners of her eyes. "But you don't need to listen to my problems."

I pulled a chair over to where Rita had been sitting, and we sat down next to each other. "I may not need to hear about what's bothering you, Rita, but I would like to. Maybe there's some way I can help."

"Would you mind putting a bullet in Lee Buchanan's head? Or maybe it's me you should shoot."

Rita proceeded to tell me what happened after she and Lee dropped me off the previous day. They returned to Red's house, and Lee shared the contents of Red's will. Apparently the old man intended to play Cupid posthumously because he left his house and half his savings to Lee and the other half of his savings along with the acreage adjacent to his house to Rita. Rita was dumbfounded that Red had provided for her, but she didn't have long to savor the moment. Lee told her he was glad his father had remembered her in his will after all she did to care for him. Then he announced that he had married a woman in Florida and planned to bring her back to Charles City County to live in Red's place.

Hearing Rita's sad tale, I felt like crying, too. Years of patience, understanding, and hope had been repaid with a brief and devastating declaration. She squandered the better part of her youth waiting for Lee to realize what most folks in these parts took for granted, that Rita and Lee were a good match. Why is it that some men, and probably some women as well, can't seem to act in their own best interest? While I knew nothing about Lee's Florida bride, I could not imagine she was a better life companion than Rita.

As I struggled to find the right words of comfort, Emory joined us. He asked Rita if she would excuse us because he needed to discuss a private matter of some urgency. I felt like asking Emory for a few more minutes to console Rita, but he seemed uncharacteristically agitated. I reached out for Rita's hand and told her I intended to arrange a dinner together so we could continue our conversation.

Retiring to the study, Emory pulled two chairs side by side and sat down heavily, as if the weight he bore no longer allowed him to stand.

"Are you feeling okay?" I asked in my physician's voice.

He informed me that he'd just been on the phone with Henry Brown.

"I can guess what he wanted," I responded. "Did you tell him about the Commonwealth Power offer?"

Emory shifted in his chair. "I decided not to tell him, but for all I know, he's already aware. I'm vexed, plain and simple. There's no way Brown can match what Commonwealth Power is prepared to offer, at least not if they're thinking of creating some kind of Riviera on the River. But how can I be responsible for Devon becoming a swanky playground?"

"How badly do you need the money?"

"You know I'm desperate, Russell. We're just running on fumes."

"Are you willing to sell to Brown, even if he can't match an offer from Commonwealth Power?"

"Honestly, I don't know. The timing stinks. Devon is all Gray has in the world. No, Devon is Gray's world. How can I sell it, especially after all she's been through?"

I wanted to tell Emory that he needed to talk honestly with Gray about these matters, but I could not turn my back on the pledge I'd given Gray in the hospital. I searched for the right words. "Is it possible that Gray is not as attached to Devon as you imagine?"

Emory's right eyebrow arched. "You know the lengths she's willing to go, Russell. How can you even suggest such a thing?"

I could not say more without betraying Gray's trust. "I'm not much help, Emory," I said, standing to leave. "Something's got to give. You belong here at Devon, but you cannot afford to stay here. It's too bad you can't bequeath Devon to some philanthropic organization in return for an agreement to let you and Gray live out the rest of your days here."

Emory reached out to stop me from leaving.

"That's an intriguing idea, Russell. Why couldn't I?"

I thought for a moment, surprised that Emory had taken my offhand remark seriously. "You'd have to find an outfit willing to maintain Devon and pay the taxes while you and Gray were alive. That could be a long time."

We walked outside. I could tell Emory was mulling over what I had said.

"Are you going to tell Brown that you're not prepared to sell?" I asked as I opened the door to my Jeep.

"I owe him that much," Emory replied, adding that he would like to help the man learn more about his ancestors. "Maybe I'll invite him down here for lunch."

Suddenly I remembered my previous day's visit to the abandoned cemetery. "Speaking of Brown's ancestors, I ran across something very interesting yesterday after we scattered Red's ashes." As I explained my visit to the overgrown burial ground and Red's deathbed request, Emory's eyes locked on mine. I could tell he wanted to make sure he got every detail. When I told him about AM's marker and the adjoining graves of Sarah and Solomon Profitt, he jumped into the Jeep and insisted I show him the place.

"I'm your friend, not your physician, Emory, but you need to calm down," I teased him as we sped off. "Remember, you're a Virginian and you can only handle enthusiasm in small doses."

For the first time in a while, a broad smile stretched across Emory's face, and he chuckled, "Sober advice, Doctor Curry."

Driving to the cemetery, Emory made me repeat everything I had seen the day before. We agreed that Brown had told us his grandfather's name was Solomon Profitt. Emory recalled the story Brown shared about Profitt being enslaved at Devon and his refusal to escape when McClellan occupied the plantation. Emory said he needed to check the farm records to see if Brown's great grandfather had been listed as taxable property and if there was any indication that he became a sharecropper at Devon after the war. Emory grew quiet, and I sensed his initial excitement might be waning.

A few minutes passed and Emory spoke up again. "The fact is that Profitt is a fairly common name in these parts. There's no guarantee, of course, that your Solomon Profitt actually was Brown's ancestor."

"The date of death, however, seems to be in the ball park," I added, hoping to keep Emory from drifting back into a funk over his finances.

"True, but it's also possible that your Solomon Profitt was an infant named after another Solomon Profitt. So many babies died soon after birth in those days. Brown might never have known about such an infant."

"That could explain why only one date was on the gravestone," I noted.

When we reached the burial ground, Emory hurried out of the Jeep before I shifted into park. I quickly followed, not recalling the last time I had been so anxious to plunge into a new adventure.

"Russell, I've driven this old road a dozen times and never realized there was an abandoned cemetery here." Emory talked as he threaded his way through the brambles, hardly noticing when they tore at his pants. "Where exactly was Solomon Profitt's grave?"

I pointed toward the far end of the cemetery.

We spent several hours combing the cemetery and clearing vegetation in order to read gravestones. Emory commandeered my pen and the only paper I had, my prescription pad, and jotted down names and dates. He told me his intention was to devote Monday morning to a search of courthouse records. Somewhere among the death notices, probate files, tax records, and other documents might be a clue to the identity of Solomon and Sarah Profitt.

As for the mysterious AM, Emory was not convinced it was an infant or stillborn birth. He knew of no local custom calling for the use of initials in such cases. We speculated on possible reasons why an actual name would not be chiseled into a gravestone. One obvious explanation could have been the cost. Another reason might have involved a desire to conceal the identity of the deceased.

As to why Red Buchanan asked Rita to tend a grave in a cemetery for blacks, Emory was clueless. But he intended to find out. So intrigued was my companion, in fact, that a proposal to break into the courthouse on Sunday would not have surprised me one bit. Emory invited me to meet him at the courthouse during my mid-day break on Monday, but I declined, indicating that I already had plans. What I did not share was the fact that my alternative plans involved a visit to Devon.

Chapter 13

REVELATIONS

May is Spring's gift to Virginia. Whatever the earth has been hiding since winter is finally revealed. Rough pastures are transformed into lush carpets. Gardens overflow with color. The temperature is ideal, mild mornings giving way to warm afternoons without the stifling humidity of July and August. Nowhere is Mother Nature more inclined to bestow her vernal blessings than along the banks of the James River. I know it sounds corny coming from a no-nonsense country doctor, but I was moved to tears by the magic of the season as I drove to Devon that bygone Monday.

Somehow the deaf Professor managed to detect that I was knocking at the front door because he greeted me curtly by stating that Mr. Emory was not at home. I felt that he did not care for male visitors when the master was away. My explanation that I had dropped by to see how Mrs. Ashcroft was doing failed to impress Edward. I was about to abandon my visit when Rita came in from the rear terrace and recognized me. She excused Edward, who acted peeved, and told me how nice it was to see me. Lowering her voice, she expressed embarrassment at her outburst the previous day and hoped I wouldn't hold it against her.

"Doc, I'm really pretty stable most of the time."

I told Rita she had no reason to apologize. What I really wanted to say, though, was how much I admired and appreciated her. Here was a woman without artifice or airs. The person you saw was the person she was. The genuine article. I couldn't help wondering what she thought of me.

Rita informed me that Emory had gone to the courthouse to do some research. I almost slipped and said I knew, but I caught myself just in time. The reason for my visit, I explained, was to see how Gray was doing. Rita said she and Gray had just finished having lunch on the terrace, then she winked and added there was enough food left over for me. I thanked her, but declined. What I wanted was to talk to Gray alone, but I didn't know how to ask without the risk of hurting Rita's feelings. She must have read my thoughts because Rita wondered if I'd mind looking after Gray for a few minutes while she excused herself.

When I walked to the terrace, Gray was stretched out on a lounge chair wearing the same sun dress she wore when I paid my first visit to Devon, only this time she didn't seem to fill it out the way she had before. I surmised Gray hadn't felt much like eating since the accident. For all her recent trials, though, she still looked damn good. "A handsome woman," my father would have declared. Gray spoke first.

"Russell, I'm afraid Emory's off to the courthouse, snooping around old records again."

"I didn't come to see Emory," I stated more bluntly than I intended.

"I see." Gray hesitated. She smoothed the wrinkles in her dress, covering her knees in the process.

"I owe you an explanation, Gray, and an apology. I should have come over sooner to see how you were doing."

"Russell, you're a busy person, for God's sake. And it's not like I'm alone. Rita's been a wonderful companion."

"The reason I didn't come by earlier had nothing to do with being busy, Gray."

She looked at me with such compassion that I suddenly felt pitiful. "Russell, I know."

The only words that came to mind at that moment seemed

hopelessly trite and trivial. Yes, Emory was a lucky man. Gray didn't need me to convey that thought. Nor was there any benefit in sharing my hope that we could still be friends. Then I realized there actually was something she needed to hear from me.

"Gray, do you remember our conversation in the hospital?"

"I wasn't that drugged up. Of course I do."

"I meant the part about why you wanted to take your own life."

Gray held a finger to her lips and gave me a schoolteacher's look of disapproval. "You promised not to say anything," she whispered.

I swore her confidence had not been betrayed, then explained that Emory believed she had tried to kill herself because she couldn't bear the thought of leaving Devon.

Gray's brow furrowed, and she asked how I knew this to be true.

After making her swear never to tell her husband what I was about to reveal, I related my conversation with Emory at the hospital on the night of her accident.

Gray admitted that there was a time when Emory's conjecture might have been valid. She dearly loved being a lady living by the River. "You'd have to have grown up the way I did to understand, Russell," she added with a gentle smile. "But you must understand, I love Emory far more than I love this place. If we have to move, we have to move."

How I had misjudged this woman. Perhaps Emory as well. I told Gray she must let Emory know how she really feels and sooner better than later. "The only reason he's hanging on to Devon," I asserted, "is because of you."

" You know that's not the only reason." Just then the screen door opened and Emory strolled out on the terrace.

"Russell, you old liar. Here I thought you were tied up today. Little did I know you intended to frolic with my bride." I detected just a hint of displeasure in his voice.

Gray interrupted to say that I had stopped by to see how her recuperation was progressing.

Emory kissed her forehead and pulled up a chair. "I had a most interesting morning over at the courthouse." He spread several photocopies of documents on the terrace table. The Emory who had just walked out of the house was not the failed farmer or the sad scion of a once great Virginia dynasty. He was the energized student of local history who came bearing something exciting to share.

"I am of the opinion," he began, dragging out the delivery on purpose to heighten our anticipation, "that Dr. Curry's Solomon Profitt is, in truth, Henry Brown's great grandfather." Emory savored the look of surprise on my face and puzzlement on Gray's, then showed us a photocopied page from a ledger of some kind.

Rita joined us at this point and reminded Gray that it was time for her nap. Gray thanked me for coming as Rita helped her up and handed her the walker. Gray shuffled over to Emory, kissed him lightly on the cheek, and told him he'd have to explain what all the excitement was about over dinner. As I watched Gray leave the terrace, I hoped she appreciated the importance of telling her husband how she really felt about selling Devon.

"See here," Emory pointed to an entry in the ledger. "John Mercer Profitt. Colored. Born to Solomon Profitt and Sarah. June 21, 1887." Emory looked at me. "Didn't Brown say his grandfather, the one who moved to Richmond, was named John Mercer Profitt?"

"To be honest, Emory, I don't recall. All I remember is Solomon Profitt."

"I'm certain he said John Mercer Profitt because I wondered at the time if he'd been named after John Mercer Langston."

I shook my head. "Who is he?"

Emory explained that Langston once rivaled Frederick Douglass as the nation's leading black spokesman. He was born a free child on a Virginia plantation, eventually going north and earning a law degree. After the Civil War, he served in various important posts, including envoy to Haiti and head of the institution that eventually became Virginia State University. Langston had the dubious distinction of being the last popularly elected black Congressman in the nineteenth century. Emory apologized for lecturing, but I marveled once again at his knowledge of historical details.

"There are lots of Profitts in these parts," I observed. "How can you be so sure the Solomon Profitt in the cemetery is Brown's great grandfather?"

"Look here." Emory pointed to another photocopy from his stack. "This is the entry in the ledger of deaths in Charles City County between 1866 and 1910. Solomon Profitt. Husband of Sarah. Died of natural causes. November 22, 1904."

I exclaimed, "That was the date on the gravestone." I could see how tracing missing relatives could grow on a person.

"I doubt whether too many Solomon Profitts who died in 1904 and were married to Sarah also had a son named John Mercer." Emory held up yet another photocopy. "There's more! This page is from the tax records for 1859. Fortunately the document was not destroyed during the Civil War, like so many other local records. See, my great grandfather's taxable property is listed in this column."

I looked where Emory was pointing. In faded handwritten script were written the first names of Emory Allen Ashcroft's chattel, including "Solomon, child." I admitted the evidence was intriguing, but added that it was impossible to tell from the entry whether or not the Solomon on the property list was the Solomon in question.

"I know, Russell. You'd make a fine historian. I realize the evidence so far is circumstantial, but I did find one additional bit of information." Emory picked up the last photocopy.

"What's this?" I asked. "It looks like some kind of contract."

"That's precisely what it is. This document was a sharecropping agreement between my grandfather, Emory Allen Ashcroft II, and Solomon Profitt. My great grandfather never would have made such an agreement with a former slave, but his son was less set in his ways. When he took over managing the farm, he apparently allowed Solomon Profitt to split the yields from farming part of the estate. The contract is dated March 31, 1873."

I admitted that Emory had located some very compelling leads concerning the identity of Solomon and Sarah Profitt. "What about AM?" I asked. "Did you run across anything that might reveal his or her identity?"

"Not a clue, I'm afraid. But Brown should be pleased to find out where his great grandparents are buried."

I thought about Henry Brown and how he might react to this news along with Emory's reluctance to sell the plantation.

"By the way, Russell, I've invited Brown to come to Devon this Friday at 11:00. I'd be grateful if you would join us once again."

It appeared I'd find out for myself how Brown would react.

<h1 style="text-align:center">Chapter 14</h1>

WHAT TO DO WITH DEVON

As I was leaving the office for Emory's meeting with Henry Brown, Grace stopped me and asked if I had heard the news about Lee Buchanan. According to her sources, Lee had driven back to Florida and intended to return to Virginia with his wife and move into Red's place. "If I were Rita," she added, "I'd probably feel like crawling under a rock. That boy doesn't deserve the likes of Rita."

The drive over to Devon went more quickly than usual. I wanted to arrive early enough to see how Rita was doing before Brown arrived. If someone had asked me why I was so concerned about Rita, I'm not certain what I would have said. Though I felt sorry for her, pity couldn't account for my solicitude. Truth be told, I was glad things hadn't worked out between Lee and Rita. My relief, I began to suspect, had less to do with Rita's feelings than my own.

"You're here bright and early," Emory said as I stepped out of my Jeep. "Slow day at the office?"

I explained my desire to catch a moment with Rita before Brown showed up. When I informed Emory that Lee planned to move into Red's place with his new wife, he replied, "Rita called this morning and said she was feeling under the weather. I told her to take the day off. Gray's getting around better."

I asked if Rita sounded distraught.

Emory looked at me, and I could tell he'd taken note of my concern. "Don't worry, Russell. She just sounded tired."

As we walked into the house, I made a mental note to call Rita and invite her out to dinner the following evening. Ever since we stayed up half the night with Red, I sensed a connection with Rita that I had not felt with a woman in a long time. The connection wasn't electric, like the spark that Gray ignited, but magnetic, like the attraction between two objects of compatible composition.

When Emory and I entered the library, Edward was arranging a side table for coffee.

"Good morning, Professor. I trust this fine morning finds you in excellent health."

"Morning, Dr. Russell," Edward replied as he laid out cups and saucers. "I didn't wake up on the wrong side of the grass, so I guess it is a fine morning." It was the first time Edward ever addressed me by name. Clearly the man could hear when he wanted to.

"Edward, you know as well as I do that the good Lord never intended for you to die," Emory offered with a benign smile. "You'll still be here..." Emory turned away without finishing his comment. Edward excused himself and left.

I waited a few moments until Edward reached the kitchen. "Are you still determined to reject Brown's offer?" I asked Emory while pouring myself a cup of coffee.

Emory stared at the portrait above the mantelpiece. "I haven't forgotten your idea, Russell. I've been contemplating going to the Association for the Preservation of Virginia Antiquities and asking if they would consider purchasing Devon."

I reminded Emory that this process could take a fair amount of time. Such negotiations don't always go smoothly. Then I asked him how long he could hold out financially.

Emory poured himself a cup of coffee and took a seat opposite my chair. I noticed his eyes were bloodshot and the skin below his eyes was puffy.

Resorting to my physician's role, I asked Emory how long it had been since he'd gotten a good night's sleep. I offered to prescribe a sedative, but we were interrupted by the sound of a car door being shut. Emory shouted toward the kitchen, "Edward, my other guest has arrived." I had never heard Emory raise his voice before.

Several hard raps on the door later, Emory concluded that Edward hadn't heard his call or else was tied up somewhere outside. As he went to open the door, Emory muttered something about Edward living in a world of his own.

"Russell, you remember Mr. Brown," Emory said as he ushered his guest into the library.

I shook Brown's hand, registering the firmness of his grip and the fact that he made eye contact. Most of the rural folks I met in the office avoided looking me straight in the eye when I greeted them. "I met you and your lawyer here several weeks ago."

"Speaking of your lawyer," Emory interrupted, "where is Mr. Allen?"

"Allow me to apologize for my ex-lawyer's unprofessional conduct," Brown replied as he took the cup of coffee Emory offered. "Apparently the man contacted at least one other party once he learned that Devon might be for sale. I expected him to be my exclusive representative."

"I guess that explains why Commonwealth Power contacted me," Emory responded as he seated himself across from Brown.

Brown admitted that he couldn't possibly match an offer from the utility giant. Then he added, "Perhaps it doesn't matter anyway. My wife has notified me in no uncertain terms that she has no intention of moving to Charles City County. She wants our son, John Henry, to attend school in Richmond. It's more than that, of course. All of her friends are in Richmond. She doesn't want to be isolated in some relic of times best forgotten, as she puts it."

I asked whether that meant he no longer was interested in purchasing Devon.

Brown turned toward Emory. "No, I would still like to realize my grandfather's dream of owning property here."

"And not just any property hereabouts, I imagine," Emory responded.

"To own the plantation where my ancestors worked in bondage would mean a lot to me," Brown acknowledged. "I cannot deny it."

"Nor would I want you to. If our roles were reversed, I suspect I'd feel much the same." Emory poured another cup of coffee.

Brown inched toward the edge of his chair. "Let me get right to the point, Mr. Ashcroft."

I waited for Emory to suggest that Brown address him by his first name, but he made no such offer.

Brown explained that his wife was perfectly willing for him to purchase Devon as an investment, just as long as the family didn't have to move there. "If you're still interested in selling Devon," he continued, "I would be willing, no, I would be pleased to have you and your wife continue to live here. I have several ideas about how to make Devon more profitable, but my main interest is seeing that people, particularly young people, have an opportunity to understand what the plantation system was all about. There's a lot of history along the James, and not just white folks' history."

I looked at Emory, and Emory looked back at me. Neither of us spoke nor did we believe we had heard Brown correctly.

Over the next hour Brown laid out a plan that reflected a significant amount of careful thought on his part. I could see why he was so successful as a lawyer. To feed the appetite for turf by the growing number of Williamsburg-area golf courses, Brown suggested converting some of Devon's fallow fields to a turf farm. Other parts of the property might be developed into a tree farm or even a vineyard. He pointed out that there were tax advantages associated with tree farms. The heart of the plantation – the mansion and dependencies – would become a living museum, a kind of rural extension of Williamsburg. The stables would be converted to a dormitory where visitors might spend weekends learning what life was like on a James River plantation. Brown stopped at this point and looked at Emory, then added, "It is my considered opinion that there is no better, pardon the expression, overseer for Devon's educational operations than Emory Ashcroft the Third."

Brown sipped his coffee and awaited a response from his obviously stunned host.

I could see Emory collecting himself. "You are quite a salesman, Mr. Brown. But what's to prevent me from taking your wonderful ideas and implementing them myself?"

"Nothing." A smile flashed briefly across Brown's face. "Except honor."

"And honor is everything, Mr. Brown," Emory responded.

"Emory, you are a true disciple of Mr. Jefferson," I added.

"Let us hope," Brown interjected, "that Mr. Ashcroft's devotion to Thomas Jefferson does not extend to the enslavement of human beings."

Before I could think of an appropriate response, Emory spoke up. "I must admit to you, Mr. Brown…"

"Please, call me Henry."

I waited for Emory to reciprocate the courtesy, but he did not.

"I must admit to you, Henry, that I fully intended to tell you that I was unwilling to make a deal for Devon, but your proposal gives me pause. I shall need to mull it over."

"And consult your wife, no doubt," Brown added.

"Of course. That goes without saying." I detected some defensiveness in Emory's response.

Brown asked Emory if he also was considering Commonwealth Power's offer.

Would Emory be coy, I wondered, or tell Brown the truth about his distaste for the Commonwealth Power proposal?

"A good poker player never reveals his hand, Henry," Emory replied with a genuine grin, but I've never been accused of being a good poker player. You have been truthful with me, I believe. You deserve the same in return. I have not pursued any proposal from Commonwealth Power, or any other entity, I might add."

I jumped in at this point to explain Emory's fear that the giant utility company's only interest in Devon involved residential development. Brown assured Emory that he had no desire to see the property on which his ancestors were born, toiled, and died subdivided into upscale home sites. "How can we honor our forebears if we destroy all the evidence that they were ever here?" Brown stated emphatically as he rose from his chair. "Will you be contacting me, Mr. Ashcroft, or should I call you, say in about a week?"

Emory told Brown that he would get in touch with him. As he escorted his guest out of the library, Emory suddenly stopped. "I almost forgot. My friend here chanced upon an abandoned burial ground off the Wild Turkey Road. I am quite certain your great grandfather and great grandmother are buried there."

Brown's eyes momentarily lit up at the news. Then his lawyer's reserve reasserted itself, and he began asking questions. I described the gravesites, and Emory discussed his search of the county records. Brown seemed pleased that his ancestors' remains had been located. I asked him whether he had any idea who AM might have been, but he just shook his head. Then he asked a curious question. "Have you checked with Edward?"

Emory eyed Brown with puzzlement. "You know Edward?"

"I should. He's my cousin. I thought you knew. His mother was Callie Profitt, my grandfather's sister." Brown explained that when his grandfather moved to Richmond, he wanted Callie to go with him. She was two years younger, and he felt protective toward her. But Callie was willful and had her own ideas. She took up with a man no one cared for. The man's father was a preacher, and Brown's grandfather never had much use for preachers or their kin. Too self-righteous, he claimed. The couple settled across the county near Elam Church, and that was where Edward was born.

Emory looked at me and declared, "I'm getting the feeling that a mystery has just been cleared up."

Now it was Brown's turn to look puzzled.

"Ever since your ex-lawyer contacted me," Emory began, "I've been wondering about the timing of your offer. I hadn't let anyone beyond the confines of this mansion know about my financial circumstances. Now I know why you thought I might consider selling Devon."

Brown looked embarrassed. "Don't be mad at Edward," he requested. "He's as attached to this place as you are. When he called to ask whether I'd consider buying Devon, he admitted being fearful you'd be forced to sell to people who'd wind up destroying the place."

Emory assured Brown that he was not angry. Just surprised. "It has dawned on me why Edward's been among the missing this morning," Emory added.

At the front door, Brown turned to Emory. "Say, Mr. Ashcroft, would you mind showing me where my grandfather and grandmother are buried?"

"I'd be delighted. And please, call me Emory."

Chapter **15**

WHAT TO DO WITH DEVON

Henry Brown's visit to the graves of Solomon and Sarah Profitt not only moved him mightily, but Emory and myself as well. As Emory put it during the drive back to Devon, "So much energy goes into building new relationships that it's easy to forget the importance of reconnecting with our forebears." It smarted to be reminded that I knew so little about my own ancestors.

When we returned to Devon, Brown thanked Emory and me for discovering the final resting place of his great grandparents and indicated his plans to make sure the abandoned cemetery was cleaned up. Emory expressed his interest in determining AM's identity as well as others who were buried there. He also volunteered himself and me to help with clean-up efforts.

After Brown departed, Emory turned to me and declared that he had some unfinished business to settle with the Professor. I reminded Emory of his promise to Henry Brown. "You insisted you were not angry at Edward."

Emory vowed that he had no intention of chastising Edward, but he admitted possessing a nagging notion that Edward knew a lot more than he'd disclosed. We searched the mansion, but failed to locate the Professor. Gray and Rita were chatting on the terrace, so Emory asked if they knew Edward's whereabouts. Rita had seen him earlier in the day when he mentioned needing to straighten up the guest house.

"I didn't know the guest house needed straightening," Emory responded as he motioned for me to follow him. Before leaving the terrace, he requested that Rita and Gray stick around until we returned because he had something important to discuss.

"You can rest assured I'm not going to run away," Gray teasingly responded.

The guest house had been built by Emory's father, Mosby, in 1934, the year Thomas went off to the University of Virginia. Mosby told everybody he required a retreat, a place to escape Azure Ashcroft's endless series of redecorating projects and tea parties. The real reason for building the guest house, though, was to provide a home for Thomas when he completed college. Mosby believed he could convince the young man to take over farm operations at Devon if he had his own place. After Thomas' tragic death on Route 29, Mosby never entered the guest house again. When the old man passed away, Emory and Gray used the place occasionally when friends visited. Rita, as I recall, stayed there a few nights when she was too tired to drive home after caring for Gray.

The guest house was set back among a grove of oaks and dogwoods that obscured it from those in the mansion. A two-story brick colonial with chimneys at each end and a grand view of the River from the back porch, the place beckoned to me the first time I saw it. In fact, I seriously considered asking Emory if I could rent it, but the uncertainties surrounding Devon's future led me to refrain from making a formal request. Besides, I was no longer sure I could endure living in such close proximity to Gray Ashcroft.

As we approached the guest house, I heard a sound like the creaking of an old floor when someone heavy trod across it. Looking at me playfully, Emory held up a finger to his lips to indicate quiet. He pointed toward the rear of the house. The creaking grew louder as we silently moved to the back of the house. There we found Edward resting in an ancient rocker on the porch.

Sneaking up so that he was barely an arm's length from Edward, Emory called out, "Have you ever seen a more industrious employee in your life, Dr. Curry?"

The Professor awoke with a startled look. I thought at the time that such a surprise for a person Edward's age could trigger a heart attack, but the man quickly regained his composure. Rising slowly from the rocker, Edward avoided looking at Emory or me, but announced, "Man needs to collect himself now and then."

Emory suggested Edward sit down again as we pulled up chairs beside him. I stared at Edward's antique face, dotted with white stubble and bisected by lines as deep as the furrows in the nearby fields, and wondered what secrets resided therein. Would he, or could he, ever express in terms that someone like me could understand all that he had seen and experienced in his long life?

Emory explained to Edward that Henry Brown visited earlier that morning and shared some interesting information. Edward continued to avoid looking at either of us. Emory kept creating opportunities for Edward to admit tipping off Brown about Devon's financial troubles, but Edward refused to rise to the bait. Finally Emory asked him point blank if he had been the one who notified Brown that the time might be right to make an offer on Devon.

"My mama didn't raise me up to be a liar, Mr. Emory. I did call Henry Brown. By now you must know we're kin. He was the only one I knew who might have enough money to buy your plantation. This place is home to me. I couldn't stand to see it taken by some bank or sold off to a stranger."

Emory looked at Edward and smiled. "You're as much a part of Devon as any Ashcroft. Probably more so."

"Then you won't be sending me out to work in the fields?" Edward responded with just a touch of sarcasm. That was the first time in my experience that the Professor revealed a sense of humor.

"Not this time," Emory laughed. "But I'm cutting your bourbon ration in half."

"On second thought," Edward said with a wry grin, "it'd be better to send me to the fields."

Emory and I burst out laughing. "I do have one more question for you," Emory added.

"I thought the Professor is supposed to ask the questions." Edward was on a roll now.

"Not in my classroom, Edward. Did you suggest to your cousin that Mrs. Ashcroft and I should continue to live here if he bought the place?"

"No, sir, Mr. Emory, that wasn't my idea. That was your wife's." Edward stopped abruptly and looked down in consternation.

"Have you just told us something you weren't supposed to?" I asked.

Edward kept staring at his shoes, but remained silent.

"I think we'll be needing to return to the big house to interrogate my wife," Emory announced. "Why don't you join us, Edward?"

Edward stated his desire to remain at the guest house so he could finish cleaning, but Emory insisted he come along. The three of us walked back to the house and found Gray and Rita sitting on the terrace knitting. Gray glanced at Edward. Rita offered to fetch some lemonade, but Emory asked her to stay put.

"Edward here has provided me with some very interesting information, Mrs. Ashcroft," Emory stated, sounding more like Perry Mason than a Virginia gentleman.

"Oh, Emory, don't be coy," Gray responded. "So now you know my little plan. Was it such a bad idea?" I couldn't imagine a woman being any more charming than Gray Ashcroft at that moment. She clearly was pleased with herself, but only because she had done something that demonstrated how much she loved her husband.

Emory made a half-hearted attempt to act wounded. "Generations of Ashcroft men have prided themselves on doing what was necessary to care for their families and their farms. How do you think it makes me feel when I must rely on my bride to avert disaster?"

"It should make you feel damn lucky," I interjected.

Gray and Rita smiled.

"You've been carrying the Ashcroft burden by yourself for far too long, my dear," Gray said as she reached up to grab Emory's hand.

"Tell me one thing," Emory asked Gray. "How did you know to contact Henry Brown?"

Gray looked at Edward and winked. "If you need information, you go to a professor. When I asked Edward who had made the offer on Devon, I didn't realize the man was his cousin."

"Mr. Edward is certainly full of surprises," Emory exclaimed as he walked over to the small serving table by the door. "I know it's a trifle early in the day, but I think all of Edward's and my wife's hard work deserves a toast."

"Bourbon before five?" I feigned disapproval.

"Now you understand why you're my friend and not my physician," Emory shot back. In the weeks I had gotten to know the man, I had not seen how truly playful he could be. It occurred to me that this aspect of his personality probably was what first attracted Gray.

"There's very little that good bourbon and a bad memory won't cure," Emory asserted as he filled five glasses with a few ice cubes and bourbon. "Two fingers worth," Emory claimed was the proper amount to pour before late afternoon. The care with which Emory approached his task reminded me of pictures I had seen of Japanese women performing the tea ceremony.

As Edward turned to go into the house, Emory walked over to him and put his hand on the old man's shoulder. "Under the circumstances, Edward, I believe you have no alternative but to join us."

Edward shook his head, and I sensed he felt uncomfortable having a drink with us, especially the Ashcrofts.

"You've worked at Devon your entire adult life, Edward."

"Not yet, Mr. Ashcroft," Edward noted.

"Very true, Edward. You're part of our small family. You know where the skeletons are hidden. It's only right that you join us in toasting the generous offer made by your cousin."

Reluctantly Edward took the glass from Emory.

Emory raised his glass. "To the future of Devon and to all who played a part in making her the great estate that she once was and will be again."

Gray followed with a toast of her own. "To my husband, as fine a man as ever walked on Virginia clay."

After toasting, Emory and I sat down. Edward, however, remained standing. There obviously were limits to how far he would go.

"Edward, before you leave, I'd like to ask you about a grave that Rita and Doc Curry found." Emory downed the last of his bourbon. "Did you know that they also found where your grandparents were buried?"

"Yes, Mr. Emory. Mr. Henry told me before he went back to Richmond. I never knew either of them. They passed before I was born."

Emory continued, "Well, right next to your grandparents' graves was another grave marked with the initials AM and dated 1874. Solomon and Sarah's graves were overgrown with weeds and brambles, but AM's grave had been kept clear. Have you got any idea of who's buried there?"

Edward admitted that he had never visited the cemetery because folks thought it was haunted. His mother wouldn't even go there to lay flowers on the graves of her own mother and father. The rumor was that a white woman had been buried in the cemetery and that her presence in a Negro cemetery had brought misfortune on the souls of the dead as well as their living kin. He didn't know if the rumor was true, but he suspected that the cemetery had been abandoned because folks believed it to be. "You know how superstitious people can be in these parts," he said.

Emory took a few moments to consider what Edward had shared. I could tell he would not rest until he got to the bottom of the mystery. "Well, we know one thing for sure. Red Buchanan asked Rita on his deathbed to care for AM's grave. If there's an answer to this mystery, it's most likely to be among Red's effects. Rita, did you get a chance to look through Red's belongings?"

Rita acted offended. "Mr. Ashcroft, I would never do that. They belong to his son, and," she added with unconcealed bitterness, "his wife."

Emory apologized and said he didn't mean to suggest that Rita had gone snooping around. "I just wondered if Red had any place where he kept family records, memorabilia, that kind of thing."

"You'll have to ask Lee," Rita replied. "He never mentioned anything to me."

"Then that's what we must do," Emory emphatically declared.

Chapter 16

A SURFEIT OF SURPRISES

I breathed a sigh of relief when Emory reached Lee by phone to ask if we could drop by. My friend was in such an agitated state that I feared he might decide to break into Red's house if no one had been at home. He asked Gray and Rita if they wanted to tag along. Gray's refusal did not surprise me, since it still pained her to walk more than a few steps., but I never expected Rita to accept Emory's invitation. Curiosity over Lee's wife presumably trumped the unpleasantness of seeing Lee again.

Before I knew it the three of us had piled into Emory's old Ford pickup and highballed over to Red's place. I kept an eye out for the sheriff, which was more than I could say for Emory. The truck rattled so much I thought the fenders would fall off. When we arrived, Emory bounded out of the cab at roughly the same instant he shoved the gearshift into park. Only when we had stopped in the driveway did I sense that Rita might be regretting her decision to join us. She remained seated after I got out of the truck, so I left the door open and joined Emory on the porch.

Lee came to the door and greeted us, then noticed Rita sitting in the pickup. He looked as if he was going to say something to her when his obviously pregnant wife waddled up beside him. He introduced Betty Sue to Emory and me. She shook hands, then looked toward the truck.

"And that's Rita Crockett. She's an old friend," Lee mumbled.

Betty Sue clearly recognized the name and shot Lee a menacing glance. "She doesn't look so old from here."

What could have boiled over into a very awkward situation was averted by Emory's determination to search through Red's effects. After bringing Lee up to date on the search for AM's identity, Emory asked him whether his father had left any documents, old letters, or other information that might be of help. Lee explained that he and Betty Sue were so busy getting settled that they had not conducted a thorough search of Red's possessions. "If anyone knows what Dad stashed away in this place, it'd be Rita," Lee suggested.

Emory excused himself and went back to the pickup. I don't know what he said to induce Rita to join us, but in a few moments he returned with Rita in tow.

Lee introduced Rita to Betty Sue. "Charmed," Betty Sue replied in a thick Southern drawl. She rested both her hands on her bulging tummy.

Emory asked Rita if Red ever shared any family archives with her. She shook her head, then added that there was a storage area behind the garage where lots of boxes had been piled up. Emory asked Lee if he'd mind investigating this area with him. Lee admitted that he'd have to clean out the place eventually so he'd be grateful for some help.

As we walked through the kitchen on our way to the garage out back, Rita exclaimed, "That's it!" Everyone turned and stared. She stood on her tiptoes and took down an object from the shelf above the kitchen window, then wiped off the dust with a dish towel. She handed it to Emory, saying, "Isn't that the Ashcroft crest?"

Emory's mouth opened, but no words came out. He turned the wine decanter around in his hand and carefully examined the etched crest. "Lee, do you know where your father got this?"

Lee shook his head and said that the decanter had sat on the kitchen shelf for as long as he could remember.

I asked the obvious question. "How on earth could an Ashcroft decanter wind up in Red Buchanan's kitchen?"

"There are any number of possibilities," Emory replied. "This decanter is part of a set of glasses and decanters that date back to antebellum days. The object could have been removed from Devon during the Union occupation. A servant might have pilfered the decanter and sold it. Lee's mother could have found this piece at a local flea market and bought it."

"Still, it's quite a coincidence, wouldn't you say?" Rita added.

"Indeed it is," Emory responded. "Indeed it is."

Setting the decanter on the sideboard, Emory led the parade out the back door and over to Red's garage. The storage shed behind the garage clearly had been an afterthought. Built out of cinder block with a sloping roof of corrugated metal, it abutted the rear of the garage and had to be entered through a side door. The door was padlocked, and the rust on the lock suggested that years had passed since anyone bothered to enter the shed. Having no idea where Red might have stashed a key, Lee said he'd grab a metal rod from the garage and pry open the lock. A few minutes later he returned with the rod and quickly snapped the lock. When the door was opened, we gazed on a storage room crammed so full of trunks, tackle boxes, containers of all shapes and sizes, fishing gear, old tools, busted lawn furniture, and spare auto parts that it was impossible to take more than three steps inside.

"What a terrible mess!" Betty Sue cried. "Your father was a worse packrat than you."

Lee explained that Red and Rachel lived through the Great Depression and couldn't part with anything. "Dad told me you never know when you might need things."

Taking charge of the operation, Emory instructed his decluttering squad to remove old furniture and everything that was unlikely to contain family records. Almost two hours were needed to clear out the storage shed and pile junk in the yard. What remained were several cardboard boxes with caved-in sides and tops dotted with mouse turds, a cedar chest that resembled a coffin, an ancient leather suitcase, and a large trunk with peeling side panels. The trunk turned out to be Rachel Buchanan's hope chest. Why she had chosen not to use the china, linens, and quilt inside will never be known. The cedar chest contained old fishing and hunting magazines and several boxes of lures, probably hand-tied by Red. The cardboard boxes fell apart when we untied them, depositing piles of old tax records on the storage room floor. When Emory picked up the suitcase, I could tell his initial excitement had waned.

The suitcase was locked. It had been wedged behind the cedar chest and under the cardboard boxes. A thick layer of red dust proved no one had opened the suitcase in years, if not decades. Lee gave Emory permission to pry it open, which he accomplished easily with a long screwdriver. When Emory glimpsed the contents, his face lit up. Inside was a Bible, various letters, some larger, legal-looking envelopes, and several framed photographs. Emory thought the suitcase should be moved to the kitchen where it could be carefully unpacked. Betty Sue wasn't keen about bringing the dirty object into the house, but Lee convinced her the contents could be important. I noticed Rita staring at Lee as he negotiated with his wife, and I guessed what must be going through her head. She was waiting for Lee to lose his temper, but he remained calm and composed.

A neurosurgeon performing brain surgery couldn't have been more careful as Emory gently removed each item from the suitcase and laid it on the breakfast table. When the contents were spread out, he first chose to examine the legal-looking envelopes. I probed the Bible, hoping to find an indication of its owner and possibly a family record of births and deaths. Lee studied the photographs.

"Look here," Lee called out. "There's a guy decked out in a Yankee officer's uniform. No wonder Dad kept this hidden. I can just imagine what his neighbors would have said."

"I'll wager he's a Melville," I offered. "In the front of this Bible is a list of Melvilles and when they were born and died."

"I'm pretty sure my great grandfather was a Yankee," Lee admitted as he asked to see the Bible. "The name Melville rings a bell, but Dad never had too much to say about our ancestors."

I speculated that the soldier in the photograph might be Elijah Melville, based on his birth date of June 21, 1828.

Lee figured that Elijah Melville would have been around thirty-three when the Civil War started. Looking at the photograph in his hand, he said, "This guy's got a full beard, so it's hard to say how old he is, but I'd guess somewhere in his thirties." Lee handed the photograph to Betty Sue.

Emory asked me when Elijah Melville died. "There's no date of death in the Bible," I replied.

"So the Bible might have been his." Emory was very much into his detective role. "Is Elijah the last entry in the Bible?"

"No, there's one more," I answered. "Catherine Abigail Melville, born May 15, 1874."

"My grandmother's name was Catherine," Lee announced. "She died before I was born. During the influenza epidemic."

"At the end of the First World War," I added. "In some places it wiped out entire families."

Rita had been a silent observer up to this point, but she suddenly blurted out a question. "Does anyone find anything interesting about Catherine Abigail Melville's birthday?"

Emory responded immediately. "You're right, Rita. It's the same year that's on the grave you found."

"The initials were AM. Do you think the C might have worn away?" she asked.

Emory acknowledged the possibility but expressed his doubts. "We would have detected a trace of a carved initial if there had been one before the AM. Besides, if this Catherine Abigail Melville was Lee's grandmother, she couldn't have died in 1874." Emory resumed studying the document he had carefully removed from the brown manila envelope. After several minutes he announced, "Ladies and gentlemen, I have here the last will and testament of Elijah Melville of New Haven, Connecticut. Seems he left everything to his only child, Catherine. It would appear, Lee, that Elijah Melville was indeed your great grandfather."

"If he left everything to your grandmother, Lee, it must mean your great grandmother died before he did," Rita conjectured.

"That's a reasonable guess," Emory added, as if he were a teacher acknowledging a particularly perceptive student.

Betty Sue asked what Catherine had inherited.

"You'll be interested to know that she inherited the land on which we now stand," Emory responded. "It's referred to as the Gaffney farm."

I asked Emory if the name was familiar to him.

"Gaffney used to be a popular name in these parts," he replied. "I'll have to check, but I believe there used to be a Gaffney who was a teamster."

"Does it say when the land was bought?" Lee asked.

Emory shook his head. "There's nothing in the will, but there are some other papers in the envelope."

A few minutes later, Emory made an announcement. "I've just finished reading a letter that must have accompanied Elijah Melville's will." Emory crossed the kitchen and grasped Lee's hand. "I believe this letter," he held it up for all to see, "informs us who AM was. And furthermore," he paused to heighten the effect, "it reveals a very curious fact. Lee and I apparently are related."

You could have heard a fly fart. Everyone looked at Emory. He just smiled and cried out, "The Ashcroft line lives on! We need a toast."

"Before we toast," I demanded, "tell us what's in the letter."

"If you insist." Emory clearly enjoyed teasing us. "It seems Elijah Melville kept his daughter Catherine in the dark about her mother's side of the family, that side being the Ashcrofts of Devon. Elijah Melville was the Union soldier who married my grandfather's sister, Abigail. The AM on the grave stood for Abigail Melville."

Emory paused to finish reading the letter while the rest of us stood in stunned silence. Then he shared additional revelations. "The reason why the grave did not record Abigail's full name is the same reason she was buried in a cemetery for African-Americans. Abigail took sick during her pregnancy with Catherine, and she never completely recovered. She and Elijah were living in Williamsburg at the time. It seems Elijah had fallen in love with Abigail when they met during the Civil War. He took a bullet during the Seven Days and was removed to Devon, which had been commandeered by General McClellan and turned into a field hospital. Abigail helped nurse Elijah back to health. He vowed to return after the war and ask her father for her hand in marriage. My great grandfather refused to condone the marriage. What's more, if she married Elijah against his wishes, he threatened to cut her off without a penny and never permit her name to be mentioned in his presence."

I recalled the story Emory had told me about the overturned birdbath in the garden.

"When it became clear that Abigail would not survive," Emory continued, "she requested that Elijah contact her father. Her dying wish was to be buried with her family at Devon. Ironically, Elijah had just bought the property on which we're standing from the Gaffneys. He had hoped to earn enough money doing carpentry in Williamsburg to build a home for Abigail near where she was born and raised. Elijah went to Devon and met with old man Emory, but he not only refused to honor his daughter's request, he warned Elijah that any Melville found on his property in the future would be shot."

"What a son-of-a-bitch," Betty Sue exclaimed, expressing what I imagine was the general sentiment in the Buchanan kitchen.

Emory explained that his great grandfather could not find it in his heart to forgive anyone associated with the army that had occupied his beloved plantation. He speculated that old Emory probably went out of his way to distance himself from Yankees because many of his neighbors suspected he had cut a deal with General McClellan in order to spare Devon.

"You mean they thought he was a traitor?" I asked.

"No one could ever prove such an allegation," Emory answered, "but folks in these parts wondered why other plantations had been put to the torch or ransacked while Devon went unscathed."

"What about the gravesite?" Rita asked.

Emory indicated that Elijah wanted to fulfill his wife's dying wish, but he realized no church in Charles City County would risk his great grandfather's wrath by allowing Abigail to be buried there. At least no church attended by white folk. When she heard what had happened, Abigail's beloved maid, Sarah, contacted her people. They consented to allow Abigail to be buried in their church's cemetery, but only if no one could identify the grave as belonging to an Ashcroft."

"So that explains the initials," Rita declared.

"Indeed it does," Emory affirmed. "And from what Elijah's letter says, fear of the Ashcrofts also led Elijah to conceal his land purchase from his daughter, Catherine. He warned her in the letter not to travel to Virginia or try to contact her Ashcroft relations. He also recommended that she hire a lawyer to dispose of the property."

"I guess she didn't heed his advice," Lee remarked.

"Must be a family trait," Rita added, trying to smile as she said it.

"If Elijah died in 1898," Emory continued, "Catherine would have been around twenty-four years old and apparently unmarried, since the will makes no reference to a husband. Back then, twenty-four was pretty old to be unmarried. I suspect Catherine had planned on taking care of her father in his later years. When he died, she probably had little reason to stay up north."

"Based on these letters to Catherine," Rita said as she displayed several yellowed envelopes, "she had just broken up with a man, a schoolteacher in New Haven, when her father took sick."

"All the more reason for her to head south," Emory interjected. "You know, the person in this mystery who fascinates me most is Sarah. According to Elijah's letter, Sarah not only made the arrangements to have Abigail buried, she also maintained the gravesite. Elijah wrote Catherine that she should not worry about her mother's grave because Sarah was looking after it."

Emory's interrogation of Edward earlier that day came to mind. Sarah was Henry Brown's great grandmother. Edward had told us that black folk stopped visiting the cemetery because they believed it was haunted by the ghost of a white woman buried there. "The rumors were right," I blurted out. "A white woman was buried there."

"When my grandmother came to Virginia," Lee observed, "she must have met Sarah."

"Perhaps Sarah was getting feeble," I suggested, "and requested that Catherine take over caring for Abigail's grave."

"Which would explain why Red eventually inherited the responsibility and passed it on to me," Rita pointed out. She turned and looked at Lee.

Lee picked up her drift. "If you don't mind, Rita, I probably should be the one to maintain the gravesite now."

"Just remember, Lee," Emory added, "Abigail Melville was an Ashcroft. I am more than willing to help. In fact, I'd like to see the entire cemetery spruced up. Who knows what else we'll find beneath the brambles and bushes?"

Betty Sue offered to make a pot of coffee, but Emory suggested something stronger. "We still need to toast the solving of our mystery and the discovery of a new relative."

Lee went to fetch some bourbon, while Emory washed out the decanter bearing the Ashcroft crest. When Lee returned with the bottle, Emory poured the contents into the decanter. Betty Sue passed out glasses, and Emory gave everyone two-fingers worth of the copper-colored elixir.

"A toast is in order, my friends," Emory said as he raised his glass. "I'm still uncertain how this decanter wound up in this kitchen, but it clearly belongs here, for today I have learned that my blood line does not end with me. You cannot imagine what a burden has been lifted from my shoulders."

"Or placed on mine," Lee responded, downing the bourbon in one gulp.

"Ours," Betty Sue corrected.

I looked at Rita, and she looked at me. I thought I detected relief in her eyes.

Epilogue

One of the principle goals of science is prediction. Which individuals are most likely to get a particular illness or wind up in jail or succeed in school? I was trained in the scientific method, but when I moved to Charles City County, I never would have predicted that my life and the lives of Emory and Gray Ashcroft, Red and Lee Buchanan, Rita Crockett, and Henry Brown would become intertwined. Such different backgrounds and experiences. Most observers might chalk it up to coincidence. We happened to be in the same vicinity at the same time. If you asked me, however, I'd say that there's a power in the universe, call it destiny or fate if you will, that functions like centrifugal force. It draws bodies toward each other. Nonetheless, individuals must take the final steps on their own. You might say we're destined to do whatever we have the courage to undertake.

It turned out that Henry Brown changed his mind about purchasing Devon. I heard several explanations. One version held that he abruptly came to his senses and realized that his dream of owning a plantation where his ancestors were enslaved might ruin him financially. Another story suggested that his wife threatened to leave him if he bought Devon. Had I been Henry Brown, I might have reasoned that a place like Devon could never really be mine, not with so many ghosts competing for occupancy rights. Still, the part of me that believes in poetic justice regretted that he failed to acquire the plantation.

You may be thinking that Henry Brown's change of heart devastated Emory and Gray Ashcroft. Not at all. Buoyed by the discovery that Lee belonged to the Ashcroft line, Emory approached him with a proposition. If Lee would sell his father's place, Emory could use the money to pay off his debts. Then he'd be free to sign over Devon to Lee and Betty Sue. They, of course, would have to allow Emory and Gray to live out their days in the guest cottage. Lee also would need to take over the management of farm operations. Emory, for his part, agreed to focus on generating revenue by conducting historical tours of Devon and renting the facilities for corporate retreats and weddings.

Emory and Gray were relieved when Lee and Betty Sue accepted the arrangement, and they were absolutely ecstatic when the couple brought Evan Elijah Buchanan into the world several months later. I am proud to say I was on the receiving end of the robust little tyke.

Gray Wagoner Ashcroft recovered fully from her car crash and resurrected her life as a grand dame of Charles City County. So tasteful and gracious were the weddings she planned and hosted that couples from Palm Beach to Philadelphia vied to land a spot on Devon's social calendar. Emory and Edward offered highly entertaining tours of Devon twice a month for the general public. They also conducted a spooky candlelight tour every year on Halloween. Each summer Emory invited thirty middle school students from across the Commonwealth to attend a "living history" camp at Devon. Part of the stables was converted to a comfortable dormitory to accommodate the youngsters. I used to enjoy addressing these summer groups on medical practices during colonial times. For my efforts I was amply rewarded with good bourbon and great friendship.

On April 16, 1995, Gray Ashcroft's homegoing was celebrated by over five hundred neighbors. Rich and poor, black and white, churchgoer and heathen all congregated on the lawn at Devon to honor one of their own. Her untimely death at age 62 had resulted from a blood clot sustained after a fall from her horse. Emory delivered the most moving eulogy I ever heard. I suspected his own eulogy might be delivered shortly thereafter.

Four months to the day following Gray's passing, Emory died quietly in his sleep. Had he been older than 77, I might have said he died of old age. His heart just stopped working. I knew, of course, that his heart actually had stopped working four months earlier. His final days were spent making certain that Evan Buchanan understood the roots from whence he grew. Emory's "Notes on a Remarkable Family" will one day, I trust, be published. I am pleased to report that Evan shared Emory's great love of history.

Several months before Emory passed, the two of us spent Saturday afternoon as we almost always did, sipping bourbon and hitting golf balls into the River. He sensed his time was almost up and asked that I attend to one request when he finally was laid to rest beside Gray in Devon's family plot. My friend wanted "Taps" to be played as his casket was lowered into his beloved Virginia soil. By this time, I had learned that "Taps" was composed in 1862 at Berkeley, just a few miles up river from Devon, during the first Union campaign to take Richmond. Emory took notice of the puzzled look on my face when he made the request and explained that this gesture was his way of acknowledging that the Ashcroft family no longer was a purely Southern clan. Then he added, "I think the time has come to return Abigail's birdbath to its upright position." He laughed, the only time I heard him do so following Gray's death, when I said, "I can hear the rumbling now from all those Ashcrofts rolling over in their graves."

Tobias finally retired and left me the entire practice. I immediately advertised for a partner, however. You see, I had come to the conclusion there was more to life than work. Rita Crockett helped me to see the light. Did I mention that Rita and I were married in the fall of 1975? Our wedding, I'm proud to report, was the first one that Gray Ashcroft arranged at Devon.

About The Author

Daniel Linden Duke was seventy-five years of age when he published his first novel, "Man Camp." Duke asserts that "the benefit of starting late in life is the relatively brief period of time remaining for negative reviews." After studying history at Yale University, Duke earned a doctorate and served as a professor at Lewis & Clark College, Stanford University, and the University of Virginia. He contributed to the field of organizational history and published in-depth histories of Fairfax County Public Schools, Manassas Park Public Schools, and his alma mater, Thomas Jefferson High School in Richmond, Virginia. The latter book examined the high school's efforts to address desegregation and court-ordered busing. "River of Dreams" reflects Duke's deep roots in the Old Dominion and his love of the ironies of history.